THE SKY ABOVE
THE ROOF

Also by Nathacha Appanah in English translation

The Last Brother
Tropic of Violence
Waiting for Tomorrow

THE SKY ABOVE THE ROOF

A NOVEL

Nathacha Appanah

Translated from the French by
Geoffrey Strachan

Graywolf Press

First published as *Le ciel par-dessus le toit* by Editions Gallimard, Paris, in 2019. First published in English in Great Britain in 2022 by MacLehose Press, an imprint of Quercus Editions Ltd, London.

Translation of "The Sky Above the Roof" by Brian Hill from *The Sky Above the Roof: Fifty-Six Poems* by Paul Verlaine, translated by Brian Hill (Rupert Hart-Davies, 1957).

This publication is made possible, in part, by the voters of Minnesota through a Minnesota State Arts Board Operating Support grant, thanks to a legislative appropriation from the arts and cultural heritage fund. Significant support has also been provided by the National Endowment for the Arts, the McKnight Foundation, the Lannan Foundation, the Amazon Literary Partnership, and other generous contributions from foundations, corporations, and individuals. To these organizations and individuals we offer our heartfelt thanks.

This is a work of fiction. Names, characters, businesses, places, events, locales, and incidents are either the products of the author's imagination or used in a fictitious manner. Any resemblance to actual persons, living or dead, or actual events is purely coincidental.

Published by Graywolf Press
212 Third Avenue North, Suite 485
Minneapolis, Minnesota 55401

www.graywolfpress.org

Published in the United States of America
Printed in Canada

ISBN 978-1-64445-225-7 (paperback)
ISBN 978-1-64445-226-4 (ebook)

2 4 6 8 9 7 5 3 1
First Graywolf Printing, 2023

Library of Congress Control Number: 2022938627

Cover design: Kimberly Glyder

Cover images: Shutterstock

Translator's Note

The original title of Nathacha Appanah's novel, *Le ciel par-dessus le toit*, will be recognized by most French readers as a quotation from the well-known poem by Paul Verlaine, "Le Ciel," written when the poet was in prison at Mons, which begins: "Le ciel est, par-dessus le toit, / Si bleu, si calme." At times the text of Appanah's novel contains words and images that echo lines from Verlaine's poem. In preparing this translation, I have turned to a fine translation of the poem by Brian Hill published in 1957. I have borrowed words and phrases from this to match those taken from Verlaine's poem that occur in Appanah's text. Here is Brian Hill's version of the poem:

THE SKY ABOVE THE ROOF

The sky above the roof—
How calm and blue!
A tree above the roof
Rocks a slow bough.

The sky-hung bell I watch
Sounds its sweet note;
The branch-swung bird I watch
Sings from sad throat.

My God, my God, *life's* there,
Unvexed, complete;
That placid murmur there
Comes from the street.

What have you done, who weep
Your endless tears?
What have you done, who weep
With youth's lost years?

I am indebted to a number of people, including the author, for advice, assistance, and encouragement given to me during the preparation of this translation. To all of them my thanks are due, notably to Nathacha Appanah, Katie Dublinski, Willem Hackman, Bertie Holloway, Robina Pelham Burn, Dave Roberts, Pierre Sciama, Simon Strachan, Susan Strachan, John and Anne Weeks, Elise Williams, and Helen Williams.

G.S.

THE SKY ABOVE
THE ROOF

I'm deep inside a place I don't want to give a name to
If I speak the real names of the things that are here
Beauty tenderness and imagination fly out of the window
But sometimes I forget
This is a bed, this is a chair, this is a washbasin
Outside there are noises of boots and keys turning in locks
Hey, I can see something out of the corner of my eye
It's a cockroach, all black and totally still
There are dark patches on the wall where the bed is attached
*   I know what these are*
I know how they get there and if I stay here long enough
*   I'll end up leaving a mark as well*
What shape would I leave on the wall
Would other people try to guess what it is
The way people in the world outside lying on the grass find
*   shapes in clouds*
They'd say look I can see
A dog an insect a snake
If only it could be something else

A sky a star a dream
Somewhere behind me a harsh voice yells
You motherfucker
I close my eyes and slowly everything sheds its name
Mine goes as well I'm gradually forgetting it
I'm nothing now but a boy from the shadows
Each sound rings out withers fades
Soon all that remains is the white noise my heart makes

Detainee 16587,
detention center in the town of C.

Once upon a time there was a country where they had built prisons for children because, in their efforts to turn these children into decent adults, that is to say people who keep to the straight and narrow, they could find no better means than prevention, taking them into care, deprivation, restriction, imprisonment, and a whole lot of other things that only take place within walls.

But then, happily, this country closed the prisons, knocked down the walls, and made a solemn promise that it would cease building such barbaric places, places where children could neither laugh nor weep. And since in this country they believe in reconciling the past with the present, they have retained one entrance gate, to act as a reminder for people who take an interest in such relics, people who believe in ghosts and stories that never die. For everyone else this is now the entrance to a fine park at the heart of the capital where they come to stroll, rest, and admire the open sky above them, calm and blue. They bring their own children there, for that is also what this country is now, a garden laid out over the tears of long ago, flowers where the dead lie, laughter on top of ancient sorrows.

Later on, since there have always been rebellious children, unhappy children, strange children, problem children, children who do terrible things, sad children, stupid children, children who have never been loved, children who do not know what they are doing, children who simply copy what the grown-ups do, this country has found other ways of healing them, adjusting them, correcting them, observing them, so that they might grow up to be more or less well-adjusted adults, capable of strolling in gardens beneath a wide open sky, calm and blue.

And yet there are still walls that enclose, walls that separate, walls that set people apart, protective walls that do not heal hearts. There are people on the outside, people on the inside, life histories waiting to unfold, life stories predetermined, accidents, random events, misdemeanors caused by bad luck. There are guilty people, innocent people, and, once more, we see a world configured like some abstract painting, one in which it is difficult to make out a friendly face, a loved one, to light upon a familiar feeling, a favorite color.

And so once upon a time in such a country there was a boy whose mother called him "Wolf." She thought this name would bring him strength, luck, natural authority, but how could she know that this boy would grow up to be the gentlest and strangest of sons and that he would end up being captured like a wild animal and there he is now, in the back of the police van, as we turn the page.

Monday morning but this is not the start of it all

Suddenly there is this strange, muffled calm, like a sheet laid over him, enveloping him completely. Through this imaginary fabric he studies the faces of the two men in uniform opposite him and sees nothing threatening about them. They are just two men coming along with him, that's all, why make a fuss, they are unclear figures, and, with his habit of finding rhymes for words inside his head, he tells himself that what is unclear is also near and quite dear. They are like clouds, like a drawing smudged with a finger, like the depths of water, like mist over the town. Behind the two men there is a window and past it a calm and blue sky speeds by, sometimes the tops of a few trees, and when the vehicle stops, the boy seeks something his eyes can fasten onto, a bird, a leaf in the wind, a power line. The things he can hear seem to him to be coming from a long way off: the sound of the engine, his own breathing, calmer now, his heart beating softly. He looks down at his hands, held fast by handcuffs (ruffs, muffs). He's waiting for something to happen because, for as long as he can remember, he has never been able to endure being shut in or restrained.

He's waiting for this thing to happen, even if it never simply "happens." In fact what occurs is an eruption, things are turned upside down, there is an explosion of yelling.

He's on guard against his heart beginning to race, he's on the alert for feelings of heat, then hot and cold and sweating, he's bracing himself for restlessness in his legs and twitching around his mouth. He's keeping a close watch on his mind, which is soon bound to be invaded by chaotic, noisy, senseless thoughts that make him feel as if there were a panic-stricken crowd inside his head.

And after that, he knows, here's what will happen next: he'll begin writhing and attempting to stand up, he'll try to voice his distress, but it will come out as gibberish and his longing to escape will only increase, he'll be desperately looking outside, twisting his head this way and that, he'll make a lunge toward the door or the bars separating them from the driver, because at such moments any fear of hurting himself no longer exists. And then the two men facing him will take out their batons to overpower him, or perhaps they'll just use their muscular arms to hold him down, he'll feel their adult weight upon him and that will be even worse. He'll start shouting and they, too, will begin barking out orders, even if they add *young man* following each word of command, because he must be pictured, this boy who looks like a twelve-year-old, his lips all bloody where he has bitten them and with big, sad eyes like those of an exotic animal. They'll all be thrown together as the vehicle drives off again at top speed, and, at this moment, they'll have started to sound the siren (iron, wire-on). And now his mind will have lost all connection with reason, he'll carry on shouting and struggling ridiculously, even though fully restrained, with his legs shackled, and all of them, the policemen, the driver, and the people waiting for him to emerge when they arrive, the nurse, the governor, the guards, and perhaps other people too, who'll have been forewarned, are all going to say *Well, this boy certainly lives up to his name,* because, let us now make it clear, this boy is called Wolf.

He goes on watching his hands and waiting, but nothing happens. There is still this silence, so soft and soothing that it could make the boy weep. He would like this moment, one in which the person he has always been no longer exists, to last a long time, because up until now he has always been tormented and uneasy, he has always wished he could shed his own skin, as some animals do at the end of winter (splinter, sprinter), to be reborn stronger, calmer, more intelligent. He would have liked his mother to be there to witness this moment and perhaps to grant him one of those rare smiles of hers, by which, for as long as they last, he is literally dazzled.

Wolf's face is smooth and open and inspires trust. During the summer he looks like a surfer with his bleached hair, his skin turning to copper, and then people often ask him *So, where are you from, really?* and Wolf does not know what to reply. He does not know his father, but when he comes across men in the street who look like him, neither

Black nor white, he wonders if he could be their son. His sister, who does not know her father either, is as white as their mother, that's all there is to it, that's where it stops. His sister, as he pictures her now, is small, she makes no noise, there's no anger in her, she whispers, she doesn't laugh, she giggles. She often smiles and, like him, she's often afraid. But that is just how he remembers her and he has grown weary of keeping memories alive, all the stories that perhaps only exist in his head, so that he ends up wondering if all those things are true or not, if that sister really existed, if that moment, with the knife and the cake, really happened, if the words he heard at that moment were really spoken.

When you talk to Wolf he looks you in the eye but often he does not hear what you are saying. His mind has strange ways of mixing up time, words, actions. He has memories of his grandfather playing the accordion, of his first day at school and the candy his sister had given him that day, and if you only knew how that sugary strawberry taste comes back to him from time to time! He has memories of a dog swimming very fast in the canal; of taking the car and driving without stopping; of the dragon on his mother's back; of the plastic Christmas tree in the attic; of his sister's face lit up by the television and the way she used to turn to him, reaching out an arm for him to come and snuggle up to her. He has memories of the black wooden elephant on Dr. Michel's desk; the smell of metal and gasoline in the yard; the hollow in the garden; his overwhelming urge to find his sister again. These scraps of recollection, pieced together, all form one single fragment of memory, with no chronology, as if all that had happened on the same day.

If you talk to Wolf he will occasionally listen to you, but most of the time he will be studying the alignment of your teeth, watching the movement of your eyelids, scrutinizing your eyes, your nose, noticing the vein pulsating on the right of your brow, the corner of your mouth twitching a little as you take time to reflect. He will be aware of the tone of your voice. After you have turned away from him he will retain a precise memory of your face and the way it moves: it is almost as if he had had a view of your skull and the complex way the muscles and tendons are attached. He could imitate you perfectly. Is that why his face seems vaguely familiar, as if it reminded you of someone other than himself, as if his face did not belong to him? Had he been an animal he would certainly have been a chameleon, but not a wolf, definitely not a wolf.

A long time ago Dr. Michel had told him that all the tests were good and he was perfectly healthy. When the doctor then turned to Wolf's mother was he aware of how the man's eyes softened as he looked at her and his shoulders slumped? Speaking a little more softly, the doctor had said to her *Don't worry, Phoenix, he's not ill*, and standing there, bolt upright, her arms folded across her chest, she had opened her mouth but no sound came out. Then she turned to Wolf and her gaze settled on him, heavy with reproaches for being what he was, bizarre, strange, foolish, but not ill. How could he recover from that gaze?

It may have been the previous day or the day before, he no longer knows. He had given an account of what he had done, the policeman had typed everything into the computer, and it was all so simple that this man (very broad forehead, little eyes that trembled, nose shaped like a ball, delicate lips, Wolf remembers those things perfectly) kept asking him *And is that all?*

It was simple and yes, that was all: Wolf had dreamed of his sister, whom he had not seen for many years, and when he woke up his sorrow lay heavily upon him, like a huge animal, and Wolf had had the idea of taking his mother's car and driving here to this town. Wolf knew that he was not allowed to drive, but he missed his sister very much, that was all. He did not have a license, he had driven carefully until he reached the edge of the town, where he had mistakenly begun driving on the wrong side of the road. And then there was all that noise, the shouting, his car in the ditch. And his panic attack, as well, after the police arrived.

That morning, or maybe just ten minutes earlier, the magistrate had given orders for him to be placed in custody in the juvenile section at the detention center in the town of C. and Wolf had experienced a feeling of relief at the naming of that town because his sister lived in the commune nearby. He had almost succeeded. He was nearly there.

Now the outlines of the town are beginning to appear against the sky through the van's rectangular window and one of the policemen says *This is it.* His voice is solemn and flat, as if he were simply uttering a thought out loud.

Wolf looks through the bars that separate them from the driver and beyond that through the windshield. The prison is not as he had pictured it. The great door is blue and the surrounding frame, shaped like an upside-down U, marked with the words "State Prison," is immaculately white. This reminds him of that poster in the tourist agency window, "Discover the Greek Islands!" with its blue dome and areas of white. Wolf feels disoriented. What is it doing here, this beauty, this color reminiscent of the sea, the sky? It must be a trap, this blue, like the smiles of people who stop at the yard in search of spare parts; like his sister's *I'll come back and fetch you very soon*; like Dr. Michel's *You're not ill*. Wolf feels his heart beginning to race, but then he catches sight of the buildings beyond that blue door. Three massive slabs with pointed roofs lined up, in order of size. It looks like a monster with three heads and, since Wolf does not like lies, he feels reassured. He has arrived at his destination.

Sunday, the mother

You need to stand in the corridor to see her.

The light is spilling into the kitchen at an angle and shining on her back. She is wearing one of those slightly old-fashioned fine cotton nightgowns that button down the front, sleeveless and sufficiently wide-cut around the upper arms to allow for movement and, because this garment is much too big for her, when she raises her arms the swelling of her breasts can be seen.

It is barely eight o'clock this Sunday morning and there is no noise here where she lives, well away from the town, away from the housing projects and the streets of single-family homes. Her home stands beside a badly maintained road that looks as if it might be a cul-de-sac but is not, because it carries on further, winding its way between tall trees, increasingly strewn with potholes that make motor traffic very difficult. Here and there it is overlaid with concrete slabs, but it goes on and on, until it cuts in two the meadow where occasionally three bay horses can be seen with coats so gleaming that they make one think of marrons glacés.

Here in springtime the road is lined with dandelions and daisies leaning over so far they brush against the surface. Once beyond the meadow, it takes an abrupt turn to the right, narrows, and is soon running beside the railway, taking you a good deal further than you might have expected.

Seen there like this, in the long strip of light, this woman could be exactly what she appears to be: the mother of a family doing last night's dishes. A woman, barefoot, gently warmed by the sun through the fabric of her nightgown and not really thinking of anything at this moment, being a little mesmerized by the crunching of the sponge, for she is one of those people who turn the tap on only once, so that all the plates and glasses, all the knives and forks are immediately immersed in foam. Seeing her from behind like this, one could picture her as someone who leads the calmest and most placid of lives, someone whose tale might be told in soothing tones, on the radio on a Sunday morning.

But the truth is otherwise. It takes the form of a bad headache that has been pounding away at her since dawn, ever since she learned what Wolf had done, and as she scrubs and scrubs away at the plates, to the point of breaking one of them, it is the inside of her head that she would really like to be scouring. She wishes she could clean everything out, so as to have the space and capacity to picture what Wolf has done, this boy who is not like other boys, it must be admitted, but exactly what it is that he has, or precisely what he is deficient in, she does not know. What she does know is that he took the car during the night and drove for seven hours, a boy who does not have a license and cannot catch a bus on his own, suffers from anxiety attacks, and can go for days without speaking. One who has magic fingers and can repair little things when they break down (hairdryer, telephone, power drill), his gaze acting like a scanner and detecting where the fault lies. He who can run around and around the house for two hours without stopping, is afraid of the hollow in the yard, and, now, does not want to see her.

Her headache seems to be confected from a thousand swarming thoughts, like a giant anthill, and when she sees that plate break into three—three separate pieces—she wonders what on earth this could signify. She would have liked to be able to read inanimate objects when they suddenly start sending us warning signals. Who was it who used to do that long ago, she suddenly thinks. What was she called, that girl with dreadlocks the color of mud, the one who lived in that old van with her three dogs? Fanny? Emilie? She used to fling down beer-bottle caps on the ground and lean over them, like a shaman, to read their "message."

Inside the head of this woman in a white nightgown a remark rises to the surface of the anthill and rings out, as loud and clear as the noise made by that plate breaking:

You will have two children, Eliette.

It is true that at the time she was called Eliette. She was fourteen, she used to hang out with friends every afternoon near the railway station and believed that one day she would discover what she was good for, find someone to whom she might be forever indispensable. Despite the general laughter that had greeted the dreadlocked oracle's pronouncement, Eliette had been secretly comforted. Wasn't this prediction, read from old beer-bottle caps, an assurance that one day the rage that thundered constantly within her would fade away? That one day she would become normal again, that she would know how to inhabit this body of hers, how, at last, to be her parents' daughter once more, the Eliette they spoke of as a memory, as a child who had died, a little girl to whom such a bright future had beckoned and who had shattered it all one day in December at the age of eleven? Her parents now regarded her with a mixture of pity and incomprehension and on a number of occasions she had thought they were going to shake her and insist on her giving them back their beloved little Eliette, now, immediately.

The woman who is no longer called Eliette rinses her hands and lays them, still wet, against her face. She tries to banish her memories, her parents' faces, the echo of the prediction made by that goth with her dogs. She needs to do something for Wolf and she has no one to advise her, because the people around her, the people she talks to, the people she likes, do not really know her. Do not know her completely. At this moment, standing at her sink where the foam is still hissing, she wishes that someone would prompt her with a response, that someone would tell her what to do, and she would listen, she promises.

She moves away from the sink, steps into the light, runs her wet fingers through her hair, crosses her fingers, and takes a deep breath. Two threads of water that had trickled along her forearms fall onto the floor and each creates a perfect little sun at her feet.

What time had the telephone rung? Three o'clock? There had been a voice informing her of a "serious offense" committed by her son, who had been arrested at exit 16 on the ring road at the town of C.: driving in the wrong direction without a license, an accident had been caused, two people in shock, possibly injured, we don't know yet, madame, luckily there's almost no one on the road at that time. Police custody, the boy will be brought before a magistrate tomorrow, most likely remanded into custody, we'll have to see, madame, that's for the magistrate to decide.

Then Wolf's voice on the telephone before she has a chance to bawl him out, because she would have bawled him out, she's certainly not the type to say my poor darling, what happened, why did you drive all that way, sweetheart, where on earth did you want to go like that, my poor poppet? Her son's voice on the telephone. *I want to see Paloma, I only want to see Paloma.*

But she knew that, she has known it for ten years, and yet she would never have thought him capable of this. The woman suddenly thinks of her own father who had made that same journey, driving all that way in the other direction, to come and see Paloma because, he, too, wanted only her. But she quickly banishes the thought. It's not the moment to go there, to make comparisons, to make connections between the dead and the living, between actions in the past and those in the present.

You need to get closer to her to see clearly.

The bicep on her left arm is surrounded by three jet-black bands, each a centimeter wide. On her right wrist there are three more, just as black, but as fine as lines drawn by a pen. A deep green strand of ivy starts beneath the ledge of her ankle bone, encircles her left ankle, twines its way up her leg, and disappears beneath her nightgown. Between her breasts, partly visible through the opening of her gown, there is a crested bird with both wings outstretched and a majestic tail. It was the first tattoo she had had done, at the age of eighteen, to inscribe there forever the name she had chosen for herself: Phoenix.

Because she does not want to think, because she cannot think, because there is only one person Wolf wants to see and that person is not herself, his mother, she swallows two sleeping pills and a glass of whisky and collapses on her bed.

It is strange how sometimes the mind resists both chemicals and alcohol, it is curious how nothing can stop it from mingling memories with desires, fears with joys, sky with sea.

Phoenix is dreaming: she's in the car with her son and he's driving. She's no longer angry. She no longer has a headache, she's laughing, and her laughter is, what do they say? Full-throated.

She can feel the back of her neck relaxing beneath the weight of her joy, and her son drives like the man he is not.

He resembles his father in what was most beautiful about his father, his honey-colored skin, his open smile. The car is speeding along the road, so smoothly, so easily! The sky is wide open above them! Phoenix doesn't know where they are going exactly, but in this dream it doesn't matter. Wolf is not at all himself in this dream . . . But it's quite the opposite. He's completely himself, in full command of his brain, his body, his words. He knows where he's going. It is a son like this that Phoenix had hoped for, which is why she gave him a name that would make him prominent, that would cause him to stand out from the crowd, a name to make him a man respected and held in awe.

Phoenix is dreaming: she's no longer in the car but in the yard, at the spot where the ground gives way and forms a hollow. A little boy and girl are asleep in the hollow. Slowly this depression is sinking deeper into the ground, subsiding like quicksand, but the children do not wake up, they remain there, clinging to one another. Phoenix yells out, but they are far away, beyond reach, she can no longer see them and then, in this dream, at the very last moment before she wakes up, she recognizes them: they are her own children.

You need to stand quite still and watch what tricks life plays on us.

The day ends with the woman in a white nightgown waking, drenched in sweat. The image of her two children vanishing into the earth is still vivid and the distress she felt in her dream is there, in the pit of her stomach, down her back, all over the surface of her head. Phoenix likes to believe she has finally come to occupy the place in this world that was meant for her, and it is far from being one that was handed to her on a plate. She is strong, she is sure of herself, she has no love of wimps or sissies, she is bringing up her son on her own, she is in her element talking about machinery with any one of the locals. She has a high tolerance of pain, she is wary of people who are too polite, and these days she never weeps. Never.

She gets up, staggers as far as the kitchen, kneels down to clear out the cupboard under the sink. There is the bottle of bleach, the floor cleaner, and the scouring powder. And, without knowing why, perhaps to get a grip on what she is doing, perhaps to give herself time to change her mind, she reads all the labels. She reaches out for the detergent capsule box that contains the letters her daughter has written to her. There were many of them during the first year, then they came less frequently. The most recent one dates from three years ago. She had wanted neither to hide them, nor to throw them away, nor yet to arrange them in order, like papers from an official document. She would have liked to bury them in the very depths of her head, beneath all other thoughts, other memories, other concerns. So she had put them in that old box under the sink, behind the detergent bottles. She opens the first letter and in the top right-hand corner, like the good scholar her daughter has always been, she has written her name, address, and telephone number.

Phoenix stands up quickly, she does not want to have time to regret her action. It must be understood that she has little patience with pauses for reflection, she is not happy when the mind, with its tortuous ways, seeks to dictate her life to her. She picks up the telephone and once more becomes the strong, self-confident woman, preparing to do what she has to do, without emotion, but when her daughter picks up with *Hello* so light, so open, as if she were happy, Phoenix remains speechless for several seconds, wondering how she might describe this voice, the voice of her child who went away so long ago, a child who trembled all the time and always spoke in a whisper. Her throat tightens but she is a woman who no longer weeps, so she swallows and asks, to make sure she has not dialed the wrong number, and so that she can hear that shimmering voice again. Yes, that's the word. Shimmering.

Paloma?

Sunday evening, the sister

Later on, perhaps, Paloma may recall that evening, and how it had very gently drawn a veil over the day, recall how she herself was that evening, recall her thoughts silently coming and going, recall how her heart, safe and warm, well shielded, was steadily pumping her blood, irrigating every nook and cranny of her body. She will catch sight of herself again at the window, a face at peace in the twilight breeze, gazing at the sky and the night as it falls, just the way she likes nights to fall.

Softly, gently.

The night melts over the day, leaving trails of pink, mauve, and orange. This sky above the rooftops looks like a shimmering piece of silk, she thinks, and it pleases her that this shimmering, which she has previously only encountered in the pages of books, occurs to her so readily.

Her flat is on the third floor of a little building set back some way from the avenue that runs through the town, but the life of the oncoming night reaches her: the murmur of the cars; the sound of the bell on the tram at the crossroads;

the electric gate in the parking lot, opening with a grinding clatter and closing with a whisper; hurried footsteps in the corridor of the block of flats; a few shouts of children at play. It is the end of spring and she knows that people of her age are outside, stretched out on the grass in parks that are now open late, strolling across the great paved squares, seated on wicker chairs on café terraces, their bodies turned toward one another, but Paloma is not like that. She keeps out of things, always on the sidelines, as if ready to slip away into a dark corner. It is a way of being that comes to her from long ago, but on this perfect evening those memories are distant. She reflects that if she had had a little balcony she would have installed a chair and a table there with a few vibrant plants and would have sat there, neither inside nor outside, and this would have been enough for her.

Standing at her window, she is aware of the melancholy that is always present at this blue hour; where does this feeling come from, she wonders, is it a blend of all the feelings of the evening, great and small, beautiful and ugly, faint and powerful?

On the table there is a bunch of anemones she had bought from the flower seller on the platform beside the tram two days earlier. Paloma had put the anemones into a pint glass because she does not possess a vase, despite the fact that she likes flowers—she prefers empty jars, chipped jugs, mustard pots. Going up to it, she notices that the center of each flower has turned darker and that around each of them there is blue dust. She leans over them, marveling at what she sees. It is certainly the first time she has noticed this change of color, although it is not the first time she has bought anemones on the tram platform, and she whispers *It's a beautiful blue.*

Softly, gently.

She is still smiling and it is the same as it was with the shimmering a moment ago. It may be a bit lame but it's a heartfelt phrase that has passed her lips and this is already something. Later on she may silently mouth those words again, to remind herself that there was a moment in her life when she was capable of talking to flowers, of saying things like that, things that make sense only at the time, the very beauty of which lies in their imperfection.

She goes back to the window, breathes in the twilight air, and, a few seconds later, the telephone starts ringing. There are people who believe that the body can sense things before they happen, but at this moment her body had alerted her to nothing, no sudden shiver, no sweating, no racing heart, nothing, and yet her telephone rarely rings. It is located at the end of the table where the flowers are. She takes three steps to pick it up.

Softly, gently.

Hello?

Her voice is open and light, a continuation of the shimmering sky and the blue of the flowers. There is a silence during which one must hold on to the image of this quiet, fragile figure who takes up so little space in the world and hug her to one's heart. This figure takes three more steps back toward the window and suddenly, at the other end of the night, as if at the other end of herself, a voice:

Paloma?

Outside the night has come plummeting down with the hiss of a sharpened blade, precisely the way it used to in the old days during her childhood in that house that always frightened her, with that horrible yard where there was a hollow. She and her brother used to play around that hollow but they always played there with fear in their hearts, in dread of tumbling into it head first. What if that hollow was really the start of a landslide? What if it was a mouth? What if it grew bigger in the night? These were all questions that left their mother unmoved because that was how she was, she would say something once and after that she was not to be pestered again. *It's just where the earth has subsided, that's all.* At the other side of the house there was the garage and the spare-parts business and it smelled of tires, gasoline, metal, sweat. And her mother, so beautiful in the midst of all that filth.

Her mouth fills with a strange kind of syrupy, slightly bitter saliva. It is her mother, that magnificent, cold, inflexible woman on the telephone. Perhaps she thinks Paloma has not recognized her hoarse voice because she spells it out:

It's me, Phoenix.

Paloma tries to regain her calm, she inhales deeply what the evening has to offer her and it is humid, aromatic. Phoenix does not ask her for her latest news, she makes no such pretense and the truth is that this is almost a relief for Paloma. So her mother has not changed. She is still the woman who does not like beating about the bush, pretense and sham, idle gossip, and those silences when you can hear the rain falling, and this evening Paloma is a little grateful to her for this. Paloma listens.

Phoenix tells her Wolf is being held by the police, that he is certain to be remanded into custody at the detention center in C., and that she is the only person he wants to see.

What freight this voice carries when she says *You're the one he wants to see, only you,* Paloma would dearly have liked to know, but her mother gives nothing away, no emotion, no prefatory remark, no word of anger, no word of fear, nothing at all that might reveal what is uppermost in her heart. Phoenix gives her a number to call as soon as possible and the address of the detention center. She repeats the address and telephone number and adds that she will have to show papers. She gives her time to go and find something to write with and Paloma lays the receiver down delicately beside the flowers. Everything is calm, Phoenix speaks the words carefully, plainly. Then, before hanging up, she adds *He took the car to come and see you he doesn't have a license,* and perhaps at that moment the delivery is a little less plain, less smooth.

Paloma hangs up and it is like a malady from the past returning, more powerful, more tenacious than ever, blotting out everything. Nothing remains of the twilight, the shimmering, the beautiful blue.

She stands there in this evening, as if on the edge of a precipice, not knowing how to act. Should she dive in head first, with her eyes wide open, or should she glide in gently?

Paloma closes the window and thinks about her grandfather who used to call her *little girl* so sweetly that it felt like a hand stroking her back. She leans her head against the windowpane and says to herself: little girl, little girl.

Years earlier, possibly the start of it all

Before Phoenix, Paloma, and Wolf, there was Eliette and it all began with her. Began? No, more like went off the rails, took a wrong turn, while up until then life had been what life so often is, neither remarkable, nor sad, one of those hard-working lives, with no great cleverness or foolishness, one of those lives spent striving for what is best, what is better, but not too strenuously all the same, for fear of attracting the evil eye.

Smile, Eliette, her parents say to her all the time and also *Come in and say bonjour, Eliette*, and when there is a dinner party at the house, *Sing "Au clair de la lune" for us, Eliette*.

Eliette wishes she could remember a time when they were like all those parents who are forever a little preoccupied, forever busy, ones who look the other way when their children are outside playing in the rain. But no such time seems ever to have existed, not in her memories, not in the photographs on the walls, nor in the stories her parents tell her. Sometimes a strange sensation takes possession of her. She feels herself leaving her body and floating above herself, she can see the top of her own head quite clearly. The part in her hair forms an abrupt angle on the apex of her head, like the corner of a triangle, before it plunges down in a straight line onto the back of her neck. She likes looking at this angle and it makes her happy: here is something that is not straight, that is not perfect, that doesn't do what it is told, something that isn't all the things she is supposed to be (straight, perfect, obedient). Eliette is still a child, her mind is filled with thoughts flying in all directions, she does not understand everything that is happening to her, all she knows is that she would like to go on floating, light and happy.

This is how things often take their course.

She is made to wear altered dresses that constrict her breathing. She is made up: a black line around her eyelids, cheeks colored pink, her eyelashes curled, her lips painted bright red. A long time is spent on her hair, it is back-combed, curled, smoothed down, sprayed with lacquer. Sometimes her mother adds a beauty spot to her right cheek. When she comes into the living room she is first of all complimented on her dress, her hair, her manners. Then comes the coaxing, *You're even prettier when you sing*, and it's no good thinking a couple of lines will do. No, Eliette has to sing the whole nursery rhyme. When she finally launches into it some eyes are closed, others open wide, their bodies reach out towards her, mouths grow round then stretch into smiles. It is a little bit of magic: the listeners are left feeling that what has been touched within them is what is most naked, most pure, most true, they feel both exposed and grateful. They realize how exceptional this little girl is, with her voice, her face, her magnetic presence, and they sense that something incredible is being born before their eyes, a destiny, the start of a dazzling journey through life. They can already picture themselves later on relating how they were there, at the very start, in a living room, in a little dressmaker's workroom, in a little house just like all the others, at the end of the allée des Pommiers.

Occasionally the women will say to themselves that perhaps she is a little too fussily done up—the bright red lips, the doe-like eyes emphasized with eyeliner, the pose at an angle, the high-heeled shoes, the hands on the hips— but this notion quickly vanishes, overtaken by the reassuring and conventional reflection that little girls love to make themselves look pretty. Sometimes the men have an odd way of eyeing her and it should not be supposed that their gaze dwells only on Eliette's clothes and her made-up face, no, these looks of theirs assault her, sully her. Their looks speak of things yet unknown to her, but she senses the violence and strangeness of them. When at the end they applaud and come to kiss her on her left cheek, which she has learned to offer in a certain way and with a certain smile, how could they, even for a moment, guess at the ball in the pit of Eliette's stomach as she stands in front of them, this thing swelling until she feels she will suffocate, a thing she feels thumping like the heart of a frightened rabbit she once held in her hands? How could they imagine that, in her bed at night, she sleeps on her stomach in the hope of squashing it flat, this ball? They would never be able to believe that sometimes she starves this thing or swallows disgusting stuff (a black banana skin from the garbage can, a spoonful of earth, a few drops of ink), in order to vomit up the disgusting stuff and, with it, the ball.

It all takes place in the living room painted yellow or in the workroom set up at the back of the house where there are the two Singer sewing machines, the dressmaker's dummy, the big mirror, and the jasmine scent that her mother sprays in every corner. Her mother says it reminds her of the Mediterranean, where they went long before Eliette was born. She had liked it all so much, the palm trees, the calm shorelines, the pebble beaches, the lapping of the water.

Whenever she starts talking about the South and lemons, her father holds his peace. He listens with an amiable smile, but nothing in the world would make him leave the plains, the green countryside, the broad plateau, the factory, and the vast beaches and high tides of the Atlantic coast.

Her parents never argue, that is their way, never one word louder than another, they take it in turn to speak, to have their days of regret, their moments of sadness. Their way of loving one another, of being together, is mildly cozy, comfortable, with no surprises.

Yet where Eliette is concerned they suddenly become animated, like moths attracted to the light, excited by feelings they find it hard to contain: pride, joy, admiration, hope, amazement. One should not hold it against them. Their daughter is beautiful, their daughter is gifted. They are not ready for it, they do not know how to deal with all the envious looks, all the compliments, their sudden popularity among friends and work colleagues.

And so her mother begins saying things like this:

You're very lucky to be born like this it's a gift from heaven smile Eliette it's a gift don't waste it take care of yourself stand up straight do your hair again cross your legs smile Eliette don't run don't climb trees don't eat sweets and say bonjour Eliette be good Eliette when I call you to the workroom you wouldn't want to make me miss orders that lady is important you know she works for the big shop in the town remember how lovely it was there she wants to take some photos of you and you're going to put on your smock dress hold your tummy in don't speak you're going to spoil your make-up sit up straight why are you crying you're not pretty when you cry take care if the wind changes you might stay like that what a horrid face tut tut tut.

And her father begins saying things like this:

Come here Eliette the manager has chosen you for the annual calendar you're very lucky Eliette there are a lot of children who'd like to be in your shoes whatever you do don't forget to smile but be nice to everyone Eliette you mustn't make people jealous you're so pretty my little Eliette darling you will say bonjour monsieur bonjour madame nicely when you go into the office aren't you lucky to be allowed into the office come here Eliette the manager has asked me if you could sing one or two songs at the end of the year concert isn't that a great bit of luck for us I'll accompany you on the accordion and we'll choose the two songs together and your mother will make a lovely dress for you and all eyes will be upon you and who knows it may be the start of a great career for the two of us ha ha ha.

Time passes and all the words they say to her form a crust over her like dead skin. Time passes and the very last thing they want to do is to harm her, oh no, quite the opposite. They want her to have every chance, to benefit from every opportunity, every possibility, they watch over her, protect her, keep her safe and they, like the others, imagine that this is just the start of something exceptional, they sense it, they dream of it.

At the library, where her father takes her every Saturday morning, Eliette reads *The Greatest Women in Our History* and the more she goes on reading, the more she feels cut down to size. Now she knows that she has done nothing exceptional. Does she possess a gift for languages, a talent for painting, can she unravel mathematical formulas, does she know several languages, can she read people's minds, can she read the future in tea leaves, does she display a courage that makes her exceptional? No, all that is beyond her and she feels terribly ashamed.

Time passes. Eliette sings, she poses, she does what she is told, and at the end people applaud.

Time passes, the dresses are still just as altered, the lipstick still as bright, and the looks she attracts become ever more insistent, harder, but her parents never notice anything at all.

In her bedroom, between her bed and her wardrobe, Eliette has made herself a little playhouse with a big sheet. Her father helped her to stretch and fold the fabric so as to make a flap that serves as a door. Sometimes at nightfall her mother and father stand on the threshold of her room, listening to her whispering inside her playhouse, not daring to disturb her. They conjure up a picture of her—a perfect figure in a smock dress, clips in her hair, her porcelain skin—based on the fairy-tale images that still linger in their minds. They picture their daughter, a princess among princesses, a doll among dolls, showing off her extraordinary beauty, walking along paths lined with flowers, swimming in limpid pools that sparkle with gold, and riding, oh yes, without a doubt, upon a white unicorn. They are convinced that these are the games with which Eliette amuses herself in her playhouse: Eliette in her make-believe garden, Eliette switching her flashlight on and off, Eliette with no secrets, no cares, no real thoughts in her head. After all, why should Eliette ever think? Is she not extraordinarily lucky to have been born the way she is? Does she not have everything she could want?

Things are going well here in this part of the town where the little detached houses have replaced the workers' cottages. In the gardens there are fruit trees, camellias, hydrangeas, magnolias, and roses. Things are going as well in the allée des Pommiers as they are in the rue des Cerises and, a little further on, the impasse des Pêchers. The children grow up and play together, they walk to school, some of the parents buy cars, other parents go away on vacation.

There is still so much to look forward to in life.

Eliette is eleven, she is wearing a long, glittering, blue dress with puff sleeves.

Her mother says:

This year I've surpassed myself just look at this satin lining and organza petticoat see the way it falls Eliette organza's extremely difficult to handle you know are you listening Eliette what are you thinking about you need to concentrate my girl.

Eliette remains silent, she eyes the scissors beside the dress, and wonders what her mother would do if then and there she were to cut the dress into pieces. Eliette has ideas like this, these days, both strange and exciting, and these ideas come to her when she is in her playhouse. Her mother often tries to make her remove that sheet stretched between the bed and the wardrobe, telling her it is unsightly, that she has outgrown it, but she refuses. She huddles in there, closes her eyes, and imagines taking down, one by one, all the photographs of her in the house, and throwing them in the canal. Repainting her room black. Going down into the town, walking, walking, and never going home again. Setting fire to her clothes, to her mother's workroom, smashing her father's accordion into a thousand pieces. What amazes her is that when she emerges she doesn't feel guilty. On the contrary, she would like to cling onto this rage, which seems to carry her off into daydreams, oh if only you could see her burning, smashing, yelling! But when she creeps out of her playhouse she reverts to being the girl who sings, poses, does what she is told, with that ball in the pit of her stomach, her face made up, her waist held in, her breasts already filling out and shame in her heart.

It will be the fourth time that she sings on stage for the factory's end of year concert and her parents smile fondly as they speculate on what Eliette has in store for them this year. The day after her first appearance on stage she caught chickenpox. On the night of the second time she had to be operated on for a sudden attack of appendicitis. Last year she had woken up on the day of the concert with a rash on her face and had to have an injection.

Her father says:

The manager has told me that there will be someone from the local paper there this evening oh I'm so proud of you my pretty Eliette darling.

Today, whatever this thing is, it comes in waves. It frightens Eliette, it's like the start of a fainting fit, but she resists because she knows it's not that. This mounting tide is made up of all her thoughts, her shame and her rage. She clenches her fists, she holds her breath, the wave starts up again. Her mother thinks Eliette is suffering from low blood sugar on account of stress, and feeds her bananas, squares of chocolate, and Coca-Cola. She thinks Eliette looks a bit peaked, makes her up more heavily than usual, and sprays her with a little too much perfume. So Eliette's face smells of rancid jasmine.

Eliette is eleven and she's waiting in the wings. Other children are singing and dancing, coming and going, laughing and crying, but she's not one of those, she has a corner all to herself because, as her mother has said, she's the linchpin of the whole concert. Her mother has gone to fetch some hairspray from the car, she said *Stay there, Eliette, I'll be back in a moment.*

There's this man who comes and tells her she'll be on in ten minutes. She's seen him before, he's been to their house before and he works at the factory as well, he's a friend of her father's, his name is Jean or Gérard, she can't remember which. He makes a habit of standing there in the living room, upright beside the clock, never taking his eyes off her. He claps in an odd way: slowly, keeping his hands together for several seconds, as if he were beating time. Jean or Gérard goes right up to her and asks *Where's your mother?*

Eliette doesn't answer, she's busy clenching her fists, breathing through her stomach, keeping at bay this thing that threatens to overwhelm her. Jean or Gérard is there in front of her. He whispers *You're very pretty, Eliette.* He takes her face in his hands and she flinches. *Hush, Eliette,* he says, and Eliette with that ball in the pit of her stomach and her organza dress says nothing. The fingers clutching her face are thick and rough, his sweat, like the sweat that clings to all the men who work at the factory, smells of metal, he reeks of tobacco and peppermint. Until that day Eliette had never realized that her head was so small that Jean or Gérard could have crushed it in his hands. Suddenly his face lunges at her, his lips are pressed against hers, he thrusts his tongue inside her mouth, it's thick, powerful and rasping, it rummages about inside her cheeks, brushes against her teeth, lingers against the roof of her mouth, and all the while, with his hands, he's holding Eliette's face quite still and it's easy enough for him. It's no more than a stolen kiss, after all, one of those things that are not supposed to happen. He'll soon forget about it. For him, you know, it means nothing.

For Eliette it is the beginning of the end.

Her mother comes running back and when she sees Eliette she exclaims *Eliette, what on earth have you done to your face? Your lipstick! Your foundation! Have you been trying to wipe it all off or what?*

Eliette stares at her mother, as she fusses over her, cleans her face with a cotton ball soaked in rose water, applies foundation, powder, blush, lipstick, and the beauty mark. There's so much welling up inside her she can say nothing. It's either powerful nausea or a great wave, she doesn't know which. All at once her mother cries out *There, that's better, now you're as good as new!*

Wearing her dress that catches the light Eliette goes up onto the stage and as she stands in front of the microphone, she feels herself leaving her body, floating above herself and there it is, that angle she's so fond of. For her, this evening, in front of all these people and that man from the local paper, who is there at her feet with his camera, it is the last night ever. Curiously, she feels a little sorry for her mother behind the curtains, and her father who is fiddling with the bellows of his accordion. It's not entirely their fault. She's aware of the audience holding its breath, just like the thing she has no name for and which, this time, she's not trying to evade. She opens her mouth and as the flood tide knocks her over, lifts her bodily, spins her about, and sweeps her down into the depths, she does not sing "La Mer," as had been planned, but begins screaming as she has never screamed before.

They are all so surprised that for a moment no one stirs. A harsh, strident, and prolonged scream, one that some of them will later describe as a howl and others will liken to a siren. People cover their ears, some of the children are afraid and others laugh. Her mother and father remain transfixed. That thing—is it a waking dream, is it somewhere in her memory, is it in her unconscious? she doesn't know—has taken her to a place where Eliette is alone. She strips off her clothes, each layer of glittering finery. She tears off her mask. She scrubs her bare skin to rid herself of the dead words that weigh heavily upon her. She spits out that bitter taste in her mouth, that smell of sweat and tobacco, her thoughts, her shame, the ball in the pit of her stomach, she cuts her hair, she spits on her name, and in this place where the frontiers are blurred she agrees with her mother: yes, now she's as good as new.

This is how the childhood of the girl who was called Eliette comes to an end and there is no reason to be sad, even though it happens like this in front of people who will never stop talking about that day with a mixture of horror and relish. There should be no regrets because it must be abandoned, this sham that is childhood, the masks need to be removed, the imposters unmasked, the abscesses lanced. All those vague yearnings toward the best, the magnificent, the better, must be set aside. There must be an end to fine words, noble sentiments, sickly sweet dreams. Now, what she will have to do one day, with bared teeth, is to carve out a place for herself in the world.

Phoenix from her ashes

Thump. Thump. Thump. This is Georges Eviard, the father of the girl who used to be called Eliette, closing the garage door, which is always coming off its hinges and which you need to bang three times for it to close properly. It is a little before seven in the evening in the allée des Pommiers and his wife is taking a look at herself in the hall mirror. With a practiced eye (we must not forget that she is a dressmaker), she takes stock of herself and does not hesitate, she discards the silk scarf. She thinks of that actress, Ava Gardner or Audrey Hepburn, she can't remember which, an elegant woman giving fashion advice in a women's magazine, who said that before going out she would look at herself in the mirror and remove one accessory. You always put on too much, said Ava or Audrey. Georges's wife has a moment of dejection, it's as if everything within her chest had suddenly given way, and she leans against a chair, lowers her head. Ava, now that's a name that would have suited Eliette better, she thinks, a name that can't be rejected. The mother of the girl who used to be called Eliette walks along the corridor, pauses in front of the door that has been repainted black. She heaves a deep sigh but it's all right, this is how it is. She has learned to live with it, black door, black walls, black make up, black clothes, and, as if this were not enough to make her grasp that she has failed, there are all the words that the girl who used to be called Eliette regularly flings at them and she has heard these well enough, she can still hear them, she can still feel them, on her skin, in her heart, in her head, in her sleep, in her dreams, here, there, at this moment, they are little teeming creatures with sharp claws.

Behind the door the floor creaks and whatever may be thought of her, her ways, her obsessions, at this moment she is a mother recognizing the sound of her child's footsteps and they are just the same as they were when she went looking for chocolate in the kitchen cupboard in the night, or when she came to get into bed with them because she had a pain in her tummy. Stealthy footsteps. The girl who was once called Eliette is walking toward the door and there she is on the other side.

On this festive evening, just two days before Christmas, what is needed is a miracle, so that, thanks to some word, some gesture, some thought, this wretched black door might open. The mother would need to say something, wouldn't she, she would need to take advantage of this silence, this hiatus, take advantage of the fact that they are once again so close, within touching distance of one another, here, at this very moment.

The mother opens her mouth but nothing comes out.

She closes it, swallows, opens it again but still nothing comes because nothing is good enough now for the girl who used to be called Eliette and who used to sing "Au clair de la lune" and whose face, on occasion, was evocative of those marble statues you find in museums. No word can find grace, no word can bring balm, no word can be sweet enough. No, nothing comes out of this mother's mouth and outside, suddenly, Georges sounds the horn. The mother closes her mouth, squeezes her lips together to make them full again, silently touches the door, and walks away. With a slight numbness in the tips of her fingers.

Thump. Thump. Thump. They are like the three knocks announcing the start of a play at the theater and the girl who used to be called Eliette sits up on her bed. Soon she will have to make her entrance on stage and what awaits her is no trifling matter, but she has written the script herself, she is word perfect, she knows every move, she has left nothing to chance. Thump, thump, thump, what did they once say? Hear ye, hear ye! Let the play begin!

The girl puts one foot down on the ground but that's funny, her mother comes up to her bedroom door and then nothing happens, the door handle doesn't turn, she doesn't knock, she says nothing, she makes no sound. What lies behind this silence? No, rather, what is it that could take the place of the silence between them, what is it that could sneak in, here, at this very moment, and render null and void what she is preparing to do? Occasionally the shrink asks her *What is it you really want, Eliette?* He goes on calling her Eliette, but she doesn't resent it because his words are not charged with emotion. Occasionally the shrink will ask her *What is it you need, Eliette?* and what comes into her mind is a window opening onto rooftops and pigeons taking flight, she thinks of the sea and herself in the sea and occasionally she talks about these things to this man and he seems a little sad and she knows he's restraining himself from going up to her and putting his hand on her shoulder, and she likes him all the more for this.

What might lie behind this silence she doesn't know because she no longer wants to hear those same words, all those I'm sorry, those I didn't know, those we thought we were doing our best, those after all we didn't kill anyone, those you had such a gift, those you were so beautiful, those you had such a great future, those if only we'd known what you were suffering. Lies! Fucking lies!

The girl is sixteen now and she can still never manage to scrub herself as clean as she would like. It seems to her as if it were only yesterday that she was dressed like a Lolita and was singing for the grown-ups. It feels as if there were still a trace of blush lingering on her face, a smear of lipstick. It feels as if her skin will never be totally cleansed of all those looks and all those words and as though she'll never be able to forget the way her head was held in his hands by that Jean, or Gérard. What can she do to be reborn?

Her mother is still there and the girl gets up. She walks stealthily over to the door, she stands at a slight angle, with her ear cocked, and perhaps she can hear her mother breathing. Indeed, perhaps she can hear the great effort this mother is making not to knock, not to speak, not to do anything. The girl who used to be called Eliette weakens a little and with a slight relaxation in the pit of her stomach, as if yielding to a gentle weariness, this thought comes to her: if her parents were to stay at home this evening, if they decided not to show themselves at the factory's end of year concert, as they always do on December 23, as they do every year, a couple united despite the scandal . . . (What scandal, a newcomer would invariably ask and would be told the story of little Eliette who was so beautiful and sang so well but who lost her head, hit the roof, cracked up totally, went off the rails, the poor little thing spent months in the hospital, and was committed several times for her violence. Oh yes it was violent, she was screaming into the microphone and she keeled over like a log of wood, she was thrashing about like a madwoman, she vomited all over the place, and it's so sad to be telling you all this about such a pretty child and her mother still makes the costumes for the little ones and her father, yes that's him all right on the stage, look, he still plays the accordion, isn't it all so sad, isn't it brave of them to keep coming every year?) Yes, if they were to abandon that whole charade, then perhaps this evening's performance might be canceled.

Who says that things are predestined, who says that we are the mere playthings of fate, and who can foretell how life will unfold?

A mother and her daughter, listening intently in silence, on either side of a black door. There are still so many possible outcomes.

But outside a horn sounds suddenly and in a moment of rage, pique, and, it must be admitted, a little sadness, the girl punches the wall with her fist.

A few minutes after Georges Eviard and his wife have driven off, a young man by the name of Tom is walking swiftly along the sidewalk, his body hugging the hedges and walls as closely as possible. Almost everyone has gone to the concert and his parents think he is in bed getting over the flu or a stomach bug, whatever. He has played his part well. I'm a ninja, he thinks with a laugh as he makes his way toward Eliette's house, moving noiselessly and swiftly, despite the weight of his rucksack. There must be no talk of ninjas with Eliette, nor must he call her Eliette. Tonight Tom is a man, he is no longer sixteen. The proof: this can of gasoline in his rucksack.

Eliette admits him through the door to her mother's workroom and his legs suddenly start shaking. He loses his balance, reaches out with his arm, and finds he has caught hold of Eliette's hand. She hauls him up bodily, with his rucksack, his can of gasoline, his delusions of ninja in the night, his fantasies of a first kiss with this magnificent and terrifying girl, her tongue mingling with his own and her inevitably silky hair that he would carry on stroking, unable to stop.

Bonsoir.

He says it slowly, the way they do in black-and-white films.

Have you got the gasoline?

Yes.

Come.

Come to me, come to my arms that I may take you completely, come to my room, come and let me show you, come and let me tell you, come that I may kiss you, first of all gently, then not gently at all, come with me.

This is not what she says when she leads him into the house, Tom knows it but he cannot stop himself, it is as if he had already crossed over to the other side of life, as if he had left childhood for good and every step he takes, following Eliette, is leading him a little further into this new world to find what has hitherto only existed in his imagination: bodies, tongues, a throbbing penis, a seething stomach, a heart swelling into something that is greater than himself, than this house, than this clean and tidy district, greater than all those dreams that, at this very moment, are floating upward out of the town.

In the kitchen she asks to see the gasoline, picks up the can, holds it up to look at it, shaking it a little, as if to check the level, then sets it down on the ground. Tom says nothing, he is gazing at her in this harsh, yellowish light and perhaps he has never seen her looking so beautiful. She has tied up her crimson hair—before that it was indigo blue and before that mauve—and this evening there is something different about her face, something that makes Tom long to walk out with her into the night, beneath the faltering moon as far as the canal, to linger there, perhaps, beside the softly, endlessly flowing water.

She speaks.

So, are you going to kiss me?

And what he had seen, just there beneath the fold of her lip, in the quivering of her nose, vanishes and her beauty returns once more, as dazzling and hard as a gemstone.

She says:

That's what you've come for, isn't it? Isn't that what you might call the price of the gasoline?

Tom says nothing, he holds out his hand, he would like her simply to take it and for them to forget this business of kissing because he senses that she is drowning. That she is adrift, and he would like to support her, keep her head above water.

The girl who used to be called Eliette looks at Tom and the effect this has on her, as just now with her mother, is like a relaxation in the pit of her stomach, she eyes the can, she eyes the hand he holds out. Tonight the silence is so deep, so perfect, and for the second time this evening another outcome is possible.

But then Tom utters the one name he must not utter and this acts as a detonator, a match, a catalyst.

Eliette.

What happens next should be told in hushed tones or forgotten, for there are things it brings bad luck to repeat.

What happens next is that Tom takes flight, putting a hand to his cheek where the girl who used to be called Eliette had slapped him with such force that his head spun around like that of a boxer in the ring.

What happens next is the fire that takes hold, first in the dressmaker's workroom, and then in the living room where in times past the little girl who used to be called Eliette would sing "Au clair de la lune." The frames around the photographs of her on the walls burn like kindling.

What happens next is that a neighbor, in bed with genuine gastroenteritis, calls the fire department.

What happens next is that at the community hall Georges and his wife hear the news. Their house has caught fire, their daughter is in the hospital. *How is she?* Georges and his wife tearfully ask the emergency room. *How is our darling little Eliette?*

Eliette? the doctor on duty replies. *She told us she's called Phoenix and let me reassure you, she's completely unharmed. It's a real miracle.*

The grandfather, when it is far too late

Here is how Georges Eviard must be pictured, this man standing at a drafty spot, close to the convenience store. Each time the automatic doors to the station concourse close, he has a brief glimpse of his own reflection, which is of no interest to him. He is wearing brown corduroy trousers, a blue shirt, a very thick gray fleece, a black cap. He knows he could remain there for hours and no one would notice him. He has always been like this, almost transparent, a fact that has never bothered him. As it happens, his cap conceals a mane of hair which, now that it has turned entirely white, would attract attention. At intervals he checks the time, at intervals he studies the arrivals screen, occasionally he takes out a little spiral-bound notebook, consults it attentively, his lips moving as if he were in the process of learning something by heart, and puts it back into his front right-hand pocket. If at any time he moves away by a few yards to check the big display board he quickly returns to where he was before, exactly the same spot. Beside the convenience store.

He had conscientiously jotted down in his little note-book what has been planned for today as soon as he had hung up, because it is never exactly the same, it seems as if Eliette decides things at the last minute. He pictures her again at the age of five when at Sunday lunch she was allowed to wear a pair of her mother's earrings. She would stand in front of the jewelry case moving the fingers of her right hand beside her right cheek, her lips pinched tight with excitement, trying on first one pair, then another, and then one more. In a flash of magical thinking Georges pictures her doing just this. Eliette on the telephone, still with that gesture of moving the fingers of her right hand rapidly beside her right cheek and, whether they were on the platform, or in the underground passage, or in the parking lot or in the station hall, she would always say Papa there's too much choice, the way she used to say Papa it's all so beautiful.

It would be so much simpler if children didn't turn into monsters.

Georges.

What needs to be said is that Georges is not alone. He has his wife, or at least his wife's voice, in his head and for the past ten years and three months she has been keeping him company, advising him, warning him, or, as on this occasion, reprimanding him with that familiar tone of voice. *Geo-orges.*

Sorry. I shouldn't have said monsters.

Georges Eviard is waiting for his granddaughter, he is a good half-hour early, but he cannot bear the idea of his granddaughter having to wait for him. He is too afraid of missing her, too afraid of her not finding her way, either here or in the life that Eliette makes her lead. Sometimes at night, with his eyes wide open, he is so convinced that hundreds of miles from there his granddaughter is also lying there in the darkness with her eyes wide open, that his heart misses a beat. He is not wrong.

In the outskirts of the town of L., in a house that looks as if it were sinking into the earth, Paloma, aged seven, likes listening to what the night has to say. The wooden floor in the corridor that leads to her bedroom creaks, the refrigerator in the kitchen at the end of the same corridor hums, and outside there is a wind that causes the chain on the entrance gate to make a grating sound. Farther off, there is a banging noise like one made by a tube hitting another metal object at regular intervals. She imagines insects resting, birds with their heads tucked under one wing, she thinks of worms, of cockroaches, of butterflies, of the horses in the distant meadow. She thinks about the hollow in the yard, the hollow that has always been there, so they say. It's only a patch of ground that's settled, that's all, her mother has told her, but in the night she imagines the hollow beating like a heart and if she listens carefully perhaps she can hear it. She thinks about the sleep of all those beings, about all the houses in darkness, she has a memory of the street-lamp that casts a perfectly round pool of yellow light on the corner at the end of the road. At this hour she has the feeling that if she didn't listen to these sounds, the world and all the things that dwell within it would collapse from loneliness. She knows what loneliness is, Paloma, this little girl who is only seven and somewhat afraid of this house, just as she is somewhat afraid of her mother, and all this is more than enough to cope with at her age. And perhaps this partly explains why she is how she is, timid and elusive, ever ready to slip away into a patch of shadow or behind a door, always on tiptoe, often holding her breath, occasionally with her body huddled up, and it may also explain, or perhaps not, why she believes that the night speaks to her.

She dreams of slipping in and snuggling up to her mother, but she is seven and already knows that this is a mad idea because her mother just isn't that kind of woman, that kind of mother. So Paloma stays in her own bed, her eyes wide open.

Georges has never liked the town but he is very fond of railway stations. This one is not too big, not yet, at least. He has the impression that these days everything that used to be on a human scale, recognizable, inoffensive, is being broken up, enlarged, transformed. Cafés, cinemas, shops, service stations, roads, it is as if everything were being done to make people feel ill at ease, to set them off wandering around and getting lost.

At the center of the station concourse there is a huge artificial palm tree surrounded by a wooden bench on which two young people are asleep, their heads resting on their rucksacks amid the noise of suitcase wheels, train horns, the whistles of train conductors, the voice from the loudspeakers; they are in the throes of a sleep so deep and innocent that Georges would like to shake them roughly and shout at them. Don't they have a train to catch, don't they have someone waiting to meet them somewhere? Nobody should sleep like that in public, don't they know that terrible things happen every day to people who doze off, who look the other way, who think they lead charmed lives and who lower their guard?

When his wife had told him that she was pregnant Georges had asked *Really?* as if talking to a child who made things up. They had been trying for many years and Georges may have ended up believing that it would never happen, he may even have gotten used to the idea as one comes to terms with a defect, a limp, a stammer. All that he wanted, he said, was that the baby should be healthy. In reality, when he said "healthy," he was thinking "normal," with no disabilities, he was so afraid that their chromosomes might be like themselves, a little the worse for wear. He went on to add, ten little fingers, ten little toes that's all I need. Boy or girl, hair color and eye color, all that was a matter of indifference to him. They had already chosen names: Eliette for a girl, after his grandmother, Jacques for a boy, after his wife's grandfather. On Sundays they used to go for walks beside the river and his wife wore an ample dress patterned with flowers that she had made herself, what did she call it?

Empire style.

Yes, an empire-style dress that slipped smoothly about her round stomach, as they walked along, arm in arm, talking about Georges' work at the factory, sometimes about the latest gossip his wife had picked up from other women who came in for fittings, talking about the baby and the future. The things they said were neither remarkable nor arrogant and their hearts were without fear, at peace.

Georges wonders how things would have turned out if Eliette had not been so beautiful. Did his wife already sense something that first day when, weary and holding the sleeping infant tenderly in her arms, she had said to him *I think we need to choose a different name.* Perhaps his wife had sensed that the name Eliette wouldn't suit her, that it was too old-fashioned, too narrow for her, and that this child, with a face like hers, with this vigor, would not live the life of an Eliette. His wife may have known from that first day that this baby was not the "normal" child they were expecting. As soon as she had given birth the nurses, the midwives and even some of the doctors came to look at "the most beautiful baby" in the hospital. The midwife had said *She's like an angel* and had lingered a long time admiring the baby. But Georges had checked the fingers and toes, had admired the perfect face with its creamy complexion and had replied, no, we'll do what we said. And so Eliette Eviard it was.

Sometimes, now, he contrives to escape from reality— Eliette is still called Eliette, she doesn't live in a dump hundreds of miles away, her body isn't covered in tattoos, she has a husband, she cuddles her daughter, she laughs, she has a job that doesn't consist of selling the filthy spare parts of cars, she has hands like her mother's, well moisturized and manicured, she doesn't have that rasping voice, doesn't make those trenchant remarks, she's not angry the whole time, she loves her parents once again—and at such moments Georges is once more fond of his daughter's name, he savors it and pictures himself calling out to her, just like that, from one end of the station to the other, where the people are coming and going in waves, and it would be like calling a flower of the field. Then he feels that the little girl she used to be is quite close to him and that little girl, dear God, that little girl, how he misses her!

A few years before, Georges had embarked on what he called a quest for the truth. He wanted to understand. He bought a tape recorder so as never to be caught unaware by a flash of memory, he wrote down everything that had to do with Eliette in a notebook. Surely he would come upon something (an event, a definitive remark, a choice, an encounter) and this thing, real, palpable and verifiable, would be the beginning of an explanation. Perhaps he thought this would be as simple as repairing little household appliances when they cease to function. Georges used to set them down on the table, remove the protective case, and examine them one bit at a time, one wire at a time, one circuit at a time, until he found what was not working. This could take hours, depending on the nature of the problem, but he was patient. Using his paintbrush with stiff hairs he liked to remove the dust from all the crevices and when everything was clean once more, when there was no longer any blockage, he would close up the device with satisfaction and plug it in again. In those days Georges still believed in stories of people being saved and things going back to the way they had been. He considered that nothing was predestined, that it was possible to triumph over adversity, and that no one was exempt from a miracle. His wife had no desire to help him, she did not even want to hear his project spoken of, as soon as he took out his tape recorder or his notebook she would leave the room. The truth must be confronted, he would tell her, and she would reply, what truth?

Yes, indeed, what truth? As he held forth into his tape recorder, bought on the cheap, he was on his own. He was on his own as he delved into his memory, for it was all about himself. Him, the father, the husband, the little accounts manager at the factory, the accordion player at parties on Saturdays. Eliette was left on the sidelines, her presence there was like that of a ghost. She moved the way he remembered her moving, like a marionette. She had the face of an angel, she lived showered in compliments, oohs and ahs, people called her princess, beauty of beauties. But was there anything that was actually about her, her alone, in that notebook, on that tape? Was there a trace of her voice? Did Georges talk about what she, Eliette, dreamed of, at night, or the things she longed for when she got up in the morning? No, what was there was only about him, there was only his truth.

The previous year he had taken the car and driven the four hundred miles all in one go because he could no longer bear being without any news of Eliette, and, above all, any of Paloma. He had stopped outside the gate and had read the sign AUTO PARTS: OPEN MONDAY TO SATURDAY and he had vainly called out *Paloma, Paloma!* He could not call out Eliette because Eliette no longer tolerated being called that. Nor could he call her by her different name, which, equally, would have been asking too much of him. Nobody had come to open up for him, even though he was convinced that he was being watched from behind the windows of that dreary house.

Was it his fault if everything had gone off the rails, if Eliette was now the way she was? Yes, yes, and again yes. His wife likes to add in her grain of salt when he is confounded but on this she is silent. Perhaps from where she speaks to him there are things she knows, perhaps she already knows what awaits them, perhaps she does not dare to tell him that, in reality, it was all their fault.

Georges is hot, he feels uncomfortable more or less all over, as if he were dragging around a body full of aches and pains. He takes off his cap to mop his brow and now it all starts. An old tramp: *Can you spare me fifty centimes?* A woman of indeterminate age with smooth features: *Do you know where the toilets are?* A young man who looks like a young woman: *Has the 17.53 train gone?* The store-keeper, who may be as old as he is: *Could you give me a hand moving this card stand to the back of the store, the casters are broken.* And Georges replies *I've got nothing, old boy; I don't know, ask at the ticket office; Yes; All right, but I can't be away from here for long.* The stand is not heavy, but it is difficult to move because it still has cards on it. When he gets back to the spot the child's train has finally arrived. All the other passengers have to leave before the children traveling alone can disembark with their accompanying adults.

Georges Eviard has to be pictured peering at the faces, stretching his neck, standing on tiptoe. His hair is a luminous white and amid the increasing grayness of the day it has an unreal look. His heart is torn between impatience and apprehension. When he finally sees his granddaughter walking towards him beside an escort clad in a red vest and senses that he can detect in her face the very same impatience and apprehension that are at work in his own heart, he suddenly cannot restrain himself.

PALOMA!

The volume of his shout surprises Georges himself, it came out much louder than it should have done, and he feels as if it had caused all heads to turn, but his embarrassment lasts barely a few seconds because Paloma is running toward him and his face relaxes, his heart relaxes, he hears himself laughing, his wife, too, is laughing inside his head and when his granddaughter hurls herself into his arms, it feels to him as if everything can be put together again and this moment, oh great heavens, this moment is quite simply perfect.

Wolf, like the animal

Dr. Michel likes to think there is nothing he cannot look in the face. Life as well as death, blood as well as milk, sorrow as well as joy. When he starts work, at the precise moment when he puts on his white coat and feels its weight, light as a feather, settling upon his shoulders, he is transformed for the better: his strides become long and lithe, his gestures confident, his voice drops a tone, he throws his shoulders back, he grows taller, and even as his brain goes on the alert, as if lit from within, his heart slows down. He is ready. He observes, he palpates, he asks questions, he responds, he passes from face to face, from illness to illness, with the same seriousness, the same distant manner. But he always takes his leave of his patients with a remark in a softer, more lingering tone of voice and Dr. Michel hopes the effect of this will be like that of a light stroke on the cheek, or on the hair. He thinks about such little details as he does about the color of his socks or the shape of his fingernails, which receive monthly treatment from a professional manicurist. Their actual effect on the patients is of little account, these details are there to protect Dr. Michel from the hurly-burly of everyday life.

The days, nights, and years pass and he maintains this same style. Some would say that he has a commanding presence, even that he is attractive; others that he is cold, unfeeling, lacking in empathy, but what does it matter, he's a good doctor. Of course, he would have liked to shine, make discoveries, publish, but he is not as good as that and he knows it. Occasionally he is greeted in the street with a discreet nod of the head or a shy smile; but people never come over to shake him by the hand or give him their news, not at all. In earlier times he used to congratulate himself on this respectful, almost timid distance which caused those whom he refers to as "people" to hold back from him. But these days, curiously, he has taken to wondering what it might be like to be one of those doctors who inspire more than gratitude or respect, to be one of those practitioners whom their patients end up becoming fond of and occasionally, not to put too fine a point on it, come to love dearly. He has seen evidence of this in the case of other colleagues (flowers, chocolates, photographs, faces that suddenly light up with abundant and infectious enthusiasm) and a good deal more often than he chooses to admit, now that he is growing old, he feels a strange emotion invading the pit of his stomach: it is not loneliness, it is not regret, it is something like a feeling that he has made a mistake. During his increasingly frequent bouts of insomnia he tries to call to mind one specific treatment, one particular patient from whom he might have derived special satisfaction, but all that comes back to him is a mass of faces and actions. A hazy, pale, rather sad jumble. During all those years what will he have really achieved? Has he once, even if only once, brought lasting consolation to the heart of a patient, comforted a soul's profound grief with anything other than tranquilizers?

When he wakes up in the morning and no sound can be heard from his flat, he has to make an effort to call to mind a familiar face (no matter whose, someone alive, someone dead, some fictitious character). Since it was clear that no one was missing him, Dr. Michel would so much have liked to be missing somebody.

It is the first Thursday in September and for the past twelve years he has been devoting one day each month, voluntarily, to the health center near the railway station. Here, at the center, the pressure of time is more intense, so many treatments to give, such a tumultuous flood of case histories of men and women, more than elsewhere. But what he has encountered here is a respect and regard that are absent from the corridors of the hospital. In the end it has been in the little touches that he has found consolation: the nurses' open smiles, the affectionate attention they pay him, the homemade cakes brought out at teatime, the patients' faces full of gratitude when he sees them, the wave of optimism that greets him when he enters the decrepit building—he hears Jeanne in reception turning toward the nurses' office and remarking with a mixture of delight and surprise in her voice *Dr. Michel is here!* In earlier times he would have found all that a little pathetic, but now he has come to admit that it is above all here, among these people, the poor, the refugees, people with no voice, single mothers, alcoholics, drug addicts, those who are less than nothing, the failed, the fallen, unfortunates from birth, casualties, that he has really felt he is of use.

When on this Thursday in September he parks in the space reserved for him in the health center's little parking lot the doctor is feeling somewhat weary. His nights are disturbed, he will hear a noise, and get up several times to check that the door is properly bolted. In this still warm weather he is wary of insects, his sheets smell of old skin, his heart never really calms down . . . It is as if something were going to happen. In the car the doctor pulls himself together. No, he is a good doctor who gives one day every month to the human community and in this his existence is already a good deal more valuable than those of thousands of others. This day will do him good, boost his morale, restore balm to his soul. He gets out of his car, takes a deep breath, and as he crisply slams the door his little bourgeois fit of depression is dispersed in the cool, clean air of the morning.

There's a woman giving birth in room number one.

Jeanne says this to him as soon as he opens the door of the health center, even before he has crossed the threshold. Jeanne is standing there in front of him, her face very close to his own. For the first time he notices the dark down around her lips and her hazel eyes. She is taller than he thought. Dr. Michel hesitates for a moment because deliveries are not allowed at the health center, that is in the regulations, and when a woman arrives here in an advanced stage of labor, Jeanne—this same woman in a state of panic before him now—immediately calls the emergency services. But Jeanne says again, in a shaky voice, as if she were afraid, *There's a woman giving birth in room number one.*

What Dr. Michel will never forget is the immense tattoo that seems to be drinking in all the light of that September morning and causing it to radiate back in explosions of green and orange throughout the room. He is literally stopped in his tracks by this kaleidoscope effect and for several seconds he has no idea what to do, with his bag, his arms, or the words that were about to come out of his mouth and suddenly found they were blocked. With Jeanne pushing him from behind, he goes into the room and realizes that it is an enormous dragon climbing across the woman's back.

It's too late to call the emergency services says Jeanne behind him and adds other things as well but Dr. Michel is no longer listening. The woman is on her knees, completely naked, her two hands pressed against the wall in front of her. Her russet hair is gathered into an untidy knot on the top of her head. She turns her face toward Dr. Michel and his heart misses a beat. This face is much too young, much too pure to be here, in this situation, to be contorted like that. Her body is much too smooth, much too milky white to be carrying that tattoo. It is something the doctor could have imagined upon the bodies of those Asian gang members you see in films. And he does not know why—he who has seen so much and likes to think there is nothing

71

he cannot look in the face—this shocks him. The young woman does not take her eyes off him, opens her mouth but all that comes out is a gurgling sound and then a cry of pain as extended and fine as a strand of liana. This is too much for the doctor and he looks away.

Beside the window there is a little girl. She is standing on tiptoe as if she were trying to see out of it better. She makes no sound, her presence is still, supernatural, like those children in horror films who see everything and know everything. Long afterward Dr. Michel will recall this frail figure, her neck straining upward. Is it possible that she could see something other than the sloping patch of land covered with yellowed scrub, the gates of the railway, the transmission towers? Was she perhaps, that morning, admiring the calm and blue sky? It is the presence of this child that shakes Dr. Michel out of his bemused state and brings him back to his work. He asks Jeanne to take the little girl somewhere else, puts down his bag, goes up to the young woman, and lowers his head to bring his face down to the same level as hers. Dr. Michel, who has until now only known and exercised distance and the maintenance of those invisible barriers between people like himself (doctors, lawyers, teachers) and people like her (tattooed like this, giving birth like this, mothers like this), reaches out with his arm and puts it around the young woman's shoulders. With his hand he gently massages her left deltoid muscle and says to her softly *I'm Dr. Michel, I'm here to help you but what you're doing is very good, mademoiselle, keep going.* The young woman tilts her head toward the doctor's face and her hair tickles his cheek, his forehead. He takes a deep breath. She smells of sweat, iron, gasoline, and, astonishingly, jasmine. Throughout his life Dr. Michel has avoided such evocative smells, smells that tell how people live, how people love, but on this particular morning it is precisely what he needs. At each contraction the young woman's head presses a little harder against his face and Dr. Michel breathes in and inhales a little of the perfume, the stench, the fragrance, the essence and—why not?— the youth of this woman. Does she speak without lying, does she go through life without trembling at the slightest sound? Does she love as if she were afraid of nothing? Does she live like a fire-breathing dragon?

Dr. Michel doesn't know, he no longer knows if there is anyone else in the room, time stands still, turns in on itself, and for him this infinity is wholly bearable. The breathing, first in short then in long breaths, the relaxation then the contraction, the prolonged moan, then silence. And still their heads pressed hard against one another.

Suddenly, in a hoarse, choking voice she says *It's coming, I can feel the head.* Dr. Michel draws back instinctively, not in order to do his work as a doctor but in order to take a better look, because he knows that during his fits of insomnia, in the course of those Sundays that stretch out before him like a gray shapeless expanse of carpet, when he feels so alone and so barren, he will recall this moment.

The young tattooed woman does all the work herself. Time, medicine, and progress do not exist, she could be in a cave, on an empty beach, she could be the very first woman in the world, what does it matter, she arches her back, crouches, pushes, draws breath, and her whole body is animated by contractions that show as little waves beneath the surface of her skin. She becomes a sea stirred up from within and behind her, beside her, Dr. Michel can only look on and take stock of his own uselessness. He is fascinated by this return of instinct, he is magnetized by the dragon, which seems to be awakening, green scale after green scale, red spark after red spark. Soon, he thinks, half-marveling and half-terrified, this young woman with her absolutely perfect face will be at one with the dragon and yes, soon she cries out the way the dragon spits fire over the crescent of her right shoulder. She stands up and, with her two hands, she catches the little boy as he slips out of her.

An infinitely sweet warmth fills Dr. Michel completely. So this is what he has been keeping at such a distance from himself, this animal truth that transforms us, that fulfills us, that goes beyond us. Is this the way in which he should have lived and loved? He carries out the routine tests on this vigorous little boy who is crying the way all newborn babies in good health should cry and at last, this is certain, he has become one of those doctors who will not be forgotten, will never be forgotten.

When Dr. Michel turns around the young woman is leaning against the pillow, she has undone her hair, and, helped by Claude, the nurse, she is putting on a white shirt. He notices another tattoo between her breasts. Her face has a timeless look about it, the effect she has on him is of a raw, animal beauty, that of women who existed long before canons, norms, fashions, it is a mythological thing, and he does not know what to do with all these unexpected notions. And with this overwhelming feeling of tenderness. He goes up to her with the baby still yelling and with one hand she stops him. *No breast.* Her voice is curt. The doctor trembles. He does not even dare lay the infant down on his mother. Claude swiftly leaves the room. Normally she is one of those women who are forever prattling away, long stories, with lots of detail, a veritable chatterbox, and Dr. Michel suspects she is the kind of woman who, when she is alone at home, does a running commentary on her own life. This morning, however, she says nothing as she hands the bottle of formula to the young woman, who first takes the baby from Dr. Michel's hands, cradles it in the crook of her arm, grasps the bottle, slips the nipple into its mouth, and turns her head toward the window. In profile she looks even more beautiful. What a woman, Dr. Michel thinks.

"What is he called, this little boy?"

"He's called Wolf."

"As in Wolfgang?"

"No. Wolf. Like the big bad wolf."

"Or like Hugo Wolf, the composer, famous for his settings of poems by Goethe and many others."

"No. Like the animal."

He signs the medical certificate (is silently thrilled over the young woman's name, Phoenix!), turns back several times, in search of something in her face, some signal that might give him permission to draw close, to come and admire, to stroke Wolf's little head, to utter a few words of congratulation, but no, there is nothing and he must move on to other patients. When he gets to the door he turns, his back straight, his shoulders relaxed, and, accustomed as he is to people thanking him, he waits for a word, a smile, but Phoenix stares at him as if she had never seen him before.

His morning is taken up with a crowd of people, but no face supplants that of the young woman. None of them has a dragon tattooed on their back, none of them has russet hair, none of them has the face of an antique marble statue. At her age already two children! A dragon across her back! Such mastery of pain and of her own body! How he would love to live more that way himself, such intensity, such darkness, even if it were only by proxy. She fascinates him and frightens him a little, it is strange, he had never known that before. And while Dr. Michel busies himself with all these other people, who are aware of how distracted and distant he is, how hurried his gestures are, while he fantasizes about this tattooed Phoenix, as if she were only there for him, there to give him an opportunity to lie to himself, to live through days that are more infernal, more thrilling, Claude is keeping a discreet eye on consulting room number one, where the half-open door enables her to observe the little girl.

She is called Paloma, as in the Spanish for "dove." She is just eleven. She is sitting on a chair and gently cradling her brother.

"That's good. Has he calmed down?"

"Yes. He's a nice little baby."

"Maybe. But he has to learn that in life it's no good being nice. You didn't say anything to the nurse?"

"No."

Claude knows that she ought to go in but something holds her back. It is as if these three were in possession of a secret that puts them under a bell jar, beyond reach. This began when she saw Dr. Michel stooping beside the young woman with the dragon on her back. Their heads were almost stuck together as if they were whispering things to one another, she was on her knees, naked. He had not put on his white coat, and had one arm around her. Claude has been working here for fifteen years, since the time when the center was still just a clinic, and she found it, yes, indecent. Dr. Michel, so cold, so distant, so snobbish on occasion, was transformed. He had quite literally shrunk. His face had puckered itself into a kind of pitiful pout, his shoulders had slumped, and he had subsequently been walking around the room like a little man transfixed by multiple emotions, his hands clasped together, his eyes staring. Claude could not get over it. Then she had learned their names: Phoenix, Paloma, Wolf, and the nurse had begun muttering to herself, as she does when she is upset or feels alone. She ought to go into the room, tell them they should spend a night at the maternity hospital, that she would arrange for an ambulance to come and fetch them within the hour. She ought to call social services. She ought to go in and check that everything is in order. But it is not just their names, it is the little girl, she is too silent, with her way of keeping absolutely still, as if she were trying to make herself forgotten; it is the way the mother had arrived that morning, imposing herself here; it is her "no breast"; it is her extraterrestrial beauty; it is this baby in that little girl's arms; it is that harsh voice, those tattoos; that shameless and utterly animal way of giving birth; it is the bewitching of Dr. Michel, just like that, at a snap of her fingers, while they, Claude and Jeanne, have never been able to extract anything from him beyond tight-lipped remarks. No, it's not right and she feels it. But all these years at the center have taught her to let things be what they are, that sometimes it's better to say nothing, to do nothing, because you never know whether what you have in your hand is a piece of fruit or a hand grenade.

"Are we going, Maman?"

"Yes, I've called a taxi. We'll be better off at home."

Claude backs away, her nurse's shoes making no noise.

When Dr. Michel returns to consulting room number one there is nobody there. He will look for her everywhere, even in the men's restroom. He will shut himself up in his little office and feel like an abandoned child. Is this to be his life on earth now? A life spent without making the slightest mark, without leaving the least trace?

Oh but surely Phoenix will talk about him to Wolf, won't she? It was Dr. Michel who brought you into the world! All is not lost, he will not be completely forgotten. Because that is how men in his situation, alone, with no child, with no family, have a chance of continuing to exist. By featuring in stories and anecdotes of family life, by displaying the aura of those who have assisted in the journey from one world to the other, of those who were present at moments of truth.

The day has almost ended and once the sun has set the cold wind heralds a damp, moist autumn. The center closes its doors and reverts to being this cube covered in graffiti set down close to the railway. *Au revoir, Dr. Michel! We'll see you next month, doctor!* There is nothing to do now the doctor reflects. He must go home, switch on a few lights, pour himself a glass of whisky, and wait for the night to offer him its ghosts with russet hair, its dreams peopled with dragons, wolves, phoenix, and doves. All he can hope for is that the sheets smell of jasmine.

The day cut in two

All three of them are sitting there at the dining room table, one at which they never have lunch or dinner, it is used for homework, papers, DIY, storage, clutter. There is even a cloth on this table, just look at that, a real linen tablecloth, probably new, that gives off a vague smell of plastic and things stored away, and on this tablecloth there is a single motif, a basket of fruit, repeated all along the edge to form a border, apples pears cherries bunch of grapes in a basket apples pears cherries bunch of grapes in a basket apples pears cherries bunch of grapes in a basket. Like that, twenty-six times.

There in the middle of the table that is covered by the new tablecloth is a cake, a Black Forest cake to be precise, waiting to be cut up and shared, but nobody is moving a finger.

There may still be time for this day not to break their hearts, those three.

If there were such a thing as magic, a glass bell could perhaps be placed over the house and yard, and beneath this bell, which would be the opposite of a prison, and which would function like those covering terrariums, they might find the means to grow, to blossom, to respect one another. Their dreams at night might be transformed into oxygen, the words they speak might lay foundations, they might be forever sufficient to one another in love.

If people and hearts could be transformed in an instant, one of those three might perhaps have performed some action there at the table that caused all other actions to be forgotten, or uttered words so sincere and gentle that, at a stroke, all words previously spoken ceased to exist.

If only such things were possible those three would not have been sitting there waiting for something finally to happen that would disrupt the onward course of time.

But it is too late for invoking, begging, wishing, for leaving the effort to change the course of one's own life to other people. On this day in winter, this day when the yard has been so nibbled by hoarfrost as to turn it into a white and spiky terrain, what each of the three of them needs to do is to reach out beyond themselves, to uproot them- selves, unaided, out of their own interior prisons.

When Phoenix got up that morning, her head as heavy as that bottle of cheap wine she had finished the night before, she knew she had to do something. She had noticed the suitcase in the corridor and was immediately seized with a violent impulse to throw up. She looked away, went into the kitchen, cut a lemon in two and squeezed the two halves into her mouth, just like that, tilting her head back- ward. The juice trickled over her face, several drops went into one eye, she said oh shit and some tears flowed, but it should not be thought that this was for the suitcase in the corridor. Phoenix no longer weeps. Her neck is creased with two lines running around it now, the thrust of her jaw is less clearly defined than before, her eyelids droop a little—it is as if time had softened the edges of her marble features, her contours of sculpted stone, the steel of her gaze, the firmness of her skin, everything that used to make her seem so unreal in the eyes of others, all that is a little eroded now and maybe this is for the best, she is less cold, less distant, quite simply less stunning. She has spread the rest of the lemon juice over her face. It stung, revived her skin, it was almost good, she rolled the seeds around on her tongue then crunched them between her back teeth. This is how she must be pictured now, this tall, tattooed woman with russet hair, still a little drunk, so sad, unmoving, as she concentrates on the bitter liquid that fills her mouth, flows down her throat.

At the end of it all there had only been herself, here on her own, with nobody to tell her what to do, to prompt her with her next line. There was only that story of hers, that of the failed little girl, the Eliette who sang in the living room and at the community hall, the Eliette who spent days and days in the hospital and needed pills to help her sleep. And then there had been that other Eliette with crimson hair, blue hair, multicolored hair, a shaved head, who had set fire to her parents' house. And after that there was Phoenix, who drank a bit, who sold spare parts, who had given birth to two children by two different men and was bringing them up on her own—so what?—and who didn't call them darling, or sweetheart, and didn't tell them to be what they didn't want to be. But that had not been enough. Damn it, how the hell are you supposed to lead it, this bitch of a life, so that it doesn't sneak up and bite you right in the middle of your daily routine? After all, Phoenix had done the complete opposite from her parents, who were forever telling her to be like this, like that, to sing, to smile. Well, she hasn't done that, she hasn't decorated their rooms with pink and blue posters, she hasn't made them put on costumes, she hasn't offered them up to the gaze of all and sundry, she hasn't bought them dolls with pretty dresses. She named them after a wild animal and a bird, to give them claws and wings, but that had achieved nothing. Her children were chock-full of emotion, they were frail and timid, they were afraid of the house, they were afraid of the hollow in the yard, they wanted her to take them in her arms, they wanted her to speak lovingly to them, and whenever she thinks back to her parents, to the person she once was, to everything she went through, it was all tightly woven, tightly wrapped around her, just like a spider's web, and she has never felt so restricted, so imprisoned, so captive.

Looking around that kitchen of hers, where nothing catches the eye, Phoenix suddenly thought of a cake. She pictured something round and substantial, something with chocolate, something with butter frosting like the ones she used to buy in the old days for the children's birthdays. Yes, a cake made by expert hands, with a mixer, a pastry chef's piping nozzles, and spatulas. Now that would be something, wouldn't it?

Ten minutes later, washed and changed, with the car keys in her hand, she had called out *I'm going shopping, I'll be back soon!*

Paloma heard her mother. What had she said? Shopping for tomorrow? What does it matter, the young woman thought, as she sat there on a chair in her room with her back straight, the way one sits in an unfamiliar room. Everything was ready, the suitcase, the rucksack with the train ticket in it. She was already dressed, all she lacked was shoes and coat. Everything was ready at the other end as well and Paloma felt as if at last she was going to join her real life, the one that had been following its course far away from her for all those years. In a week's time she would be starting college. She had been awarded a full scholarship and while waiting to rent a room she was going to stay with her grandfather. She had dreamed of this moment for so many years. She must not falter now.

Paloma looked at her brother as he slept and she knew that she, too, slept like that, in the fetal position, knees to chest, his hands together in prayer under the pillow. How many such things do they have in common, he, the strange little boy with the golden skin, and she, the young woman preparing to leave home? From where she was she could hear his regular breathing and occasionally a sigh, a whispered word—perhaps this was the echo of the voice he spoke with in his dreams? Since he had learned that she was going away he had got into her bed every night and clung to her. He said nothing, he simply hung on with all his might.

Paloma—and let us not forget how she is sitting bolt upright on the edge of the chair, let us not forget how little space she occupies on the earth—could now have left her room, made a slow tour of the house, letting her hand brush against the walls where no picture frame had ever hung, made herself a coffee in the old French press, picked up some object in her hand, weighing it there gently and holding it to her nose, looked at some books she would not be taking with her, remembered her childhood, recalled a particular event—a birthday party, a dinner, an evening spent with the family, whatever it might be—and run through it in detail in her head, who had done what, who had said what, and felt both sad and grateful, felt herself finally ready. Yes, Paloma could have done things like that, which people do when they know they'll be doing it for the last time, but she didn't want time to slow down, she didn't want to create new memories for herself, to be stored away in that corner of the brain labeled "the last time," she just wanted to leave.

Paloma had looked at her watch, it was five past eight, and thought, still three hours to go. From the abrupt way Wolf had sat up in his bed she'd known that this was not a good sign. There's absolutely no point in trying to guess what is going on in Wolf's head when his face looks as if it were under water, his features are blurred, his gaze is cloudy. There's no point in asking questions, there's no point in telling him to calm down, and above all there's no point in touching him at such a time, he'll begin crying out as if you had hurt him. Paloma knew all that. She had gotten up from the chair, she had opened the door to her room and said *Look, Wolf, it's open*, and sometimes that's enough for him to calm down, but not today, it seems.

Wolf is not ill Dr. Michel says at each monthly visit. *He's quite simply unable to manage his stress* and when he says *quite simply* Paloma sometimes feels like flinging a chair at his face.

"Quite simply," this is it: a little boy of seven with an urge to escape from himself, whose thoughts cannot control his body, there being too many of them, misshapen and contradictory.

"Quite simply," this is it: crises several times a year, set off by an excess of something, by not enough of something, who knows, and, today, by his sadness at knowing that his sister will no longer be there.

"Quite simply," that is it: a little boy who will run around and around the house even if it is cold, windy, or pouring with rain, and when you put it like that there's nothing to it, is there? Just a boy running around, but Wolf runs to the point of exhaustion, to the point of nausea, until his legs give way, until his thoughts (that are too many, misshapen and contradictory) retreat into the depths of his brain, and then he can collapse and wait for his sister or his mother to carry him into the house, wash him, take care of him, feed him, set him down in front of a cartoon or put him to bed.

*

So there it is, this cake on which the packaging spells out that it has been "transformed in France and assembled in our workshops." There is this table, laid, this new tablecloth, bought at the last moment. There is this day to be gotten through, but first of all, thinks Phoenix, whose heart is fluttering like that of a little bird that has fallen out of a tree, something must be said, isn't that right? Something unique, something true, something that comes from the heart and has nothing to do with sense or logic. Something that quite simply is.

Phoenix looks at her children and she repeats in her head, these are my children, because on so many occasions they seem remote from her, as if she were looking at them through dozens and dozens of panes of glass.

Paloma is eyeing the cake with a frown. Wondering perhaps if this could be a trap, if it contains something threatening that will blow up in their faces any minute now. She moves her chair closer to that of her brother without taking her eyes off the cake.

Wolf looks at his mother with that penetrating attention he often has, as if he could see your brain working, the thoughts coming and going.

Suddenly Phoenix knows what she is going to say and the story she has to tell is both extraordinary and familiar. She has never spoken about it to her children, never thought of doing so, and they have never asked her about it. And yet it is as if this story has been there from the start, from a very long time ago, as if it had been following them everywhere, free as the wind, waiting for the three of them to come to a halt one day like this one, in silence and uncertainty.

This is the story:

"I wonder what tales these walls could tell, if they could speak to us. Things are rarely what they seem and it's true, you know, this house, who'd think of falling in love with it, saying when they saw it, hey, I could live a good life here, I can just see myself with my kids here? Who could imagine flowers, trees, a swing in this yard, with a little playhouse at the bottom of it? I remember the first time I saw it. It made me think of those houses in fairy tales, where witches or outlaws live, you see what I mean? There were weeds everywhere, some of them came up to my waist. I thought I'd just arrived at the end of the world and that was exactly what I wanted. I came here with a boy called Noah. That's not his real name but Noah suited him well. He'd been born here, just like you two. I met him in the street, he had a guitar and he was playing a few chords. It was as if he was alone in the world, just strumming away, you know. He was busking in the street, that's for sure. We met again and chatted and got on well and he told me about his house that was waiting here for him. That's what he said, yes, just like that, he had a very soft voice, you had to get close to him to hear what he was saying. He used to say, my house is waiting for me, and, I don't know how to explain it, maybe I never will, but each time he said this my heart began to beat a little faster. He had a place of his own, he had somewhere in the world where he belonged. I'd never known such a feeling and it was one I envied. When I think back to my parents' house . . . It was pretty, everything was charming, as my mother used to say, there was a garden where my mother grew flowers with names I no longer remember, there was the factory, and there was the dressmaking workroom. That could have been fine . . . of course . . . it was fine for lots of other people but not for me. I couldn't bear that life, I felt like a wind-up doll in a plastic box that was kept on a shelf and now and then it was taken out, the key was turned and it danced and sang and everyone applauded. There are times when I'd like to say that I've found out who was to blame, because I often think about those days. Who's the guilty party? Who made me what I am, who put those ideas into my head that gave me all those desires, dreams, nightmares? I don't know and I suppose I'll have to live with it now.

"We were good together, Noah and me, and one day I came here with him. The moment I saw it I loved this house, it was like meeting someone who'll never lie to you, never pretend to be what they're not. We worked away like madmen, cutting back the weeds, clearing, cleaning, I'd never worked like that before in my life. The more tired I became, the more it let light into my mind and slowly what had been there before began to fade away. Noah knew a bit about engineering and little by little we put together our auto parts business. I learned from him. With him. What I want to tell you is that this house did me good, it protected me, it never betrayed me. Even when Noah left, even when things were rocky . . . Yes, I know what people say, I know about the hollow in the yard, I know this road is a mess,

I know you think it's the back of beyond here . . . But what I'm telling you is that this house is yours. You can go around the world, you can say what you like about it, but it'll always be here, waiting for you, and later on you'll understand what I'm saying. You'll see things the way I do."

Again, silence.

Sometimes it would be good, wouldn't it, to fathom the precise nature of words: the impact they make on people's souls, the insidious effect they have on people's thoughts, how long they last, whether they sweeten hearts or make them bitter. Are they going to lodge somewhere in the brain and one day pop up again, who knows why or how? Will they have an immediate effect, provoke anger, sadness, amazement? Will they be misunderstood, will they cause confusion?

Phoenix cannot endure the silence that continues around the table. She reaches for the knife to divide up this wretched cake and as she leans forward a little it gives off a smell of alcohol. Then she remembers that there are cherries in brandy in a Black Forest cake and if there's one thing that she and her children loathe, this is it. She doesn't hesitate, cuts three slices, and slides them onto plates. Then Paloma stands up and, as she does so, Phoenix knows that her words have been wasted.

"Is he my father, this Noah?"

"What? What's that got to do with what I've just said?"

"I'm asking you. Is he my father?"

"Sit down, Paloma. Eat your cake."

"It's a Black Forest cake, it's got alcohol in it. I don't like that. Wolf, don't touch that cake."

"Of course he can. Wolf, you can eat it."

"No, he can't. He took his medication this morning because he had a crisis, and, what's more, he loathes Black Forest cake. I loathe Black Forest cake. Of all the cakes that exist you've chosen the one we loathe. What kind of mother would do that?"

"Paloma!"

"So, is he my father, this Noah who busked in the street?"

"I was talking to you about this house, I wanted to tell you how much—"

"How much you love it. Yes, we got that. Is that man my father? Answer me, Maman. Just for once, answer me. Where is he now? Is he dead? Did he go off and leave me? What did you do to make him clear off? Did you like this house more than you liked him?"

"Paloma, sit down and eat this fucking cake."

"No. I won't eat this fucking cake, I want you to answer me. Is he my father or not, this Noah?"

Phoenix stands up. Paloma is already on her feet and it is like a scene in one of those old films where two characters are eyeballing one another, as if for a duel. They have walked around the table and Phoenix is taller than Paloma, stronger, more russet-haired, more beautiful, more tattooed, more likely to fly off the handle. But today this does not cross Paloma's mind. She loathes her mother as much as she loathes Black Forest cake and she yells *Answer me!* Phoenix raises her hand, the hand still holding the knife used to cut up the cake, and, dangling from the blade, there is a fragment of cherry like a fragment of flesh.

The promise of this day is brought to an end here by a great yell uttered by Paloma and Phoenix, an enraged chorus, a dumbfounded chorus, a yell, driven by the sight of blood, by that gesture frozen in midair and by all that has not come to pass.

Paloma rushes to her room and grabs the suitcase and her rucksack, yelling, as if spitting things out, and her words seep into Phoenix's heart like a bitter draft.

I hate you, I'll never come back to this rotten hovel, this shithole.

She sets her things down on the threshold, goes back to Wolf and whispers in the boy's ear *I'll come back and fetch you very soon* and her words seep into his heart like a sweet draft.

The girl dragging her suitcase along the road full of potholes, weighed down by her rucksack, her face streaming with tears. The light above her becomes metallic, the wind grows stronger. Paloma has the strange feeling that if she turned around she would see something terrifying.

The woman with russet hair who is left there, stock still, with her knife, incredulous. What to do with it! Cut the day into two to make a before and an after? Cut the umbilical cord? Cut the ties that unite us and the knots that go with them?

93

She looks at Wolf and realizes that from now on she is absolutely alone.

Outside a fine beam of sunlight falls onto the yard and Wolf is the only one to notice it. He imagines himself going out there and holding up his hands, cupped like a bowl, at the precise spot where the sunbeam falls.

Ten years later, Monday

So many things can change in ten years, can't they?

There is Paloma who has never set foot in her childhood home again. She has not forgotten her brother, she dreams about him regularly, but time has erased her feelings of anguish and guilt at having left him there. She has written frequently, she has several times tried to telephone, but then weariness gained the upper hand. She was always the one who was making the effort, trying, saying sorry, offering to come and visit, but how many times is it possible to be like that, on bended knee, with a bowed head, waiting for a reply? Paloma works now. There is brightness in her life but in somewhat pastel shades. She wishes she could get carried away occasionally. She wishes she could be like the others, impulsive, yelling their heads off, kissing, hungry to live out their youth, but she cannot manage it. She tries hard to live in the here and now a little bit, just enough, but not too much, and it is as if she were a trainee at living her own life, still waiting to pass the test. And, pending something better, this life is perfectly bearable.

There is Phoenix who has had a path laid down all around the house so that Wolf can run and run. She watches over him, she guides him as best she can, she loves him in her own way, and knows that this is not enough. There is that straight stretch of road cutting through the meadow and that is where Phoenix has taught him to drive and occasionally this tall woman with russet hair weakens a little and allows Wolf to put his foot down. They have not forgotten Paloma either, but life at such moments, when their bodies are pressed back against the seat, when the speed calls forth the dormant child within them, life at such moments is perfectly bearable.

Over ten years there are changes in the wider world. Islands disappear, hills collapse and settle, villages are swallowed up by desert, and towns nibble at the countryside. There is joy and there is also death that carries people away. There is forgiveness, beautiful words are exchanged at dawn. Ten years. But there are still places like the one where Wolf finds himself now.

When the policeman opens the van there is a woman wearing ballet flats that make her look like an Asian woman with tiny feet, although she is tall and Black. She is flanked by two uniformed guards with very black, well-polished boots that make them look like soldiers with big feet. The woman eyes him kindly and remarks, neither to Wolf nor to the others but perhaps to herself, *They're sending us little kids now.* Wolf looks beyond her, and sees this vista, the color of mud, everything with a look of mud, slipping away and unfolding before his eyes, buildings, doors, gates, windows, steps, and when he is fully out of the van and the handcuffs have been removed, he looks up at the sky and that, too, is mud-colored. Perhaps this is a parallel world in which all color has been removed, to punish them more severely and now this boy, named after a predatory animal, silently begins to weep.

But this is a place where lingering in the courtyard, looking at the sky, and weeping is not permitted. Wolf allows himself to be led: a door, a staircase, the clerk's office where he signs papers, and where a man talks to him without really looking at him. In this office, where there's a plant with bright red flowers standing on the windowsill, words go astray. Wolf is given a detainee number and stares at this number for several seconds, not because he recognizes it, but because he realizes that he must now learn it by heart, that this number will from now on take the place of his name, and that if anyone here in the detention center asks him *So who are you really?* he will no longer be thinking about those men, neither Black nor white, one of whom might be his father, here he will reply *I'm detainee 16587.*

Is it extraordinary that this number should comfort him, calm his heart, slow down the twitching in his legs? Is it extraordinary that for the moment he should feel as if he has been liberated from the burden of his name? He is still being led, his name is spoken, his detainee number. Occasionally someone says *Hi, how goes it?* But they are clearly not speaking to him. People say getting there, people say juvenile section, occasionally they say *Where are you having lunch today?* But they are clearly not speaking to him. Someone says search, someone says shower. The guard with very fair hair who says *Hello young man* searches him with hands smeared in ointment that do not hesitate and that's the best way, isn't it? There's no mistaking the nature of what he's doing, you can't say it didn't happen, you can't pretend. He hands over his wallet, his telephone, he would like to keep a piece of paper on which are written his sister's contact details (given reluctantly by Dr. Michel) and he is allowed to keep it, with *Right, OK*. He would like to keep his watch, but he is refused with *No, that stays here*. Wolf takes a shower and he thinks about his mother who used to make him wear flip-flops (cops, slops) at the swimming pool, so as not to pick up any filthy infection, she used to say. He looks down at his feet submerged in lukewarm water, a few wisps of foam mingled with dirt cling to his ankles, he feels his heart starting to beat faster and because he cannot start running here he rounds off his shower with ice-cold water. He knows several tricks for stopping his body taking control: running, ice-cold water, hurting himself, holding his breath. Wolf puts his clothes back on, the ones he has been wearing since Friday night.

Someone says getting there, someone says juvenile section, they repeat his detainee number. There are so many doors, it's such a maze. It's a beehive with all its dozens of cells linked to one another by a gate or a door. It should not be thought that all the places where people are locked up in this country have electronic doors that open with a buzz, a beep, or a click. This is not a place that tries to fool you into believing it is anything other than a prison. There is shouting here from those who are locked up and shouting from those who are guarding them. The confused sound of this shouting bounces off the walls. There is the noise of the bunch of keys at the belt, that of the lock, that of the system of bolts, that of a door opening, then slamming shut, boots, the crackling of voices on two-way radios.

So Wolf walks along past all the looks surveying him, indifferent, occasionally cold. At a certain moment he is given what they call a kit and he reaches a strange area. It is like a large octagonal airlock chamber from which several corridors lead off. There is blue here and yellow there. It reeks of cabbage, sweat, metal, stale breath, and if such feelings had a smell it would reek of sadness, fear, confusion, anger. When Wolf looks up he can see the transparent roof, two floors above. A daylight filters in through it that is beige (sage, cage). If there were not all these gates and doors, these bolts, these two transparent offices where he can see surveillance cameras, if there were not these guards, if there were not these nets between each floor, you might think you were in the concourse of a railway station with a glass roof and you might call this space an atrium.

Two more flights of stairs. He walks along the corridor. To his left a cell with a closed yellow door, a stretch of dirty wall, cell with closed yellow door, dirty wall; to his right this net made of thick rope, caked in dust, which stops people from jumping off. No, if they jump it stops them from falling, which is not the same thing.

In front of an open cell he is told *Here it is*. The guard asks him to open up his kit: a sheet, a blanket, a bar of soap, a toothbrush, a pen, two envelopes, some underclothes, a roll of toilet paper, a booklet, *I Am in Prison*. Wolf stands at the center of this rectangular room. A little desk, a simple bed separated from a washbasin by a partition. He is truly at the center, he can feel that all these things are there, within reach, he also feels they are all looking at him.

The guard for the juvenile section, a man so ordinary that in the outside world he could pass as the father of a family, an elder brother, a kindly uncle, or the proprietor of a local grocery store, lingers for several more seconds, then his radio crackles and he says *The meal will come soon, then you'll have exercise, that's compulsory.*

He closes the door.

Wolf makes his bed, not thinking about anything. Between the moment when he left the van and now, his heart has been closed. Perhaps it has learned how to do this during those long years when he missed his sister, those many times when he hoped for something more from his mother—a little affection, just a hand lingering on his shoulder, in his hair, a passing kiss, just like that, a gentler look, oh, hardly anything—those days spent alone at home waiting, running, waiting again.

He puts the bar of soap, the toilet paper, and the booklet side by side on the bed. He stares at them for a long time until these objects are stripped of their original meaning. He moves them a little closer to one another and there is a kind of solace in seeing these inanimate objects nestling close together. Outside, beyond the bars (stars, cigars), there is a courtyard strewn with scraps of paper, strips of cloth, plastic bottles, and little black bags. He hears *Hey, new guy, got any cigs, what's your name?*

Detainee 16587 thinks about that poem, learned when he was at school, the one about the sky above the roof, but it's not the same thing. He thinks fleetingly about his mother, then his sister, but he puts such thoughts behind him. There is a survival instinct coming into play within him, of the same kind as those that tell him to run or to thrust his head under a trickle of cold water, and this new instinct is instructing him to forget his heart, to avoid his feelings. The entirety of his mind and body is gathered in, concentrated within the four walls of his cell. He's waiting for the meal, and the exercise, he's keeping a close watch on his skin, and his thoughts, he's keeping his fear at bay with his feet on the ground. He takes a deep breath (*from the abdomen* Dr. Michel used to say) and at the age of seventeen, all that's quite enough, isn't it?

Monday night, the first
of all those nights

His mother and his sister know that Wolf is spending the night in prison, even if the correct names for it is detention center, but what difference do correct names make when there are bars on the windows, a metal door with a spyhole, and all the other things that are only there within walls? Each of them is lying in bed, both are trembling at knowing him to be alone. They get up. They try to picture what it's like to be spending the night in lockup at the age of seventeen, but no one can really imagine what the nights are like in places like that.

Paloma listens to the well-loved town noises. She inhales the night air in gulps, but a febrile sensation overtakes her, the feeling that she is being watched, followed, spied on. She cannot stop herself from going into all the rooms. The kitchen, the living room, the bathroom, opening all the doors wide, checking the windows and finally her bedroom. Is it extraordinary for this room to seem unbearable to her tonight, is it extraordinary for guilt, that monster with its honeyed tones, to be mounting within her (*he wanted to see you, he drove all those miles for you, what did you whisper in his ear, do you remember, of course you remember, it's because of you that he's spending the night in prison, he's only seventeen, he's your brother and you abandoned him*)? Paloma would like to spring out of herself, to uproot herself from her own body. She puts on her shoes and goes out. Outside she starts running, she is panting, breathing heavily, she almost falls but she carries on, she's thinking of Wolf and how he always used to run, to calm himself, to forget himself, and tonight, for her, too, all that remains is that illusion of escaping from the world, from herself.

Phoenix has already had several drinks, but this has made no difference to her distress, her anger, her disarray. Without really thinking, she picks up the telephone, dials Paloma's number, is not surprised that she has this at her fingertips because, despite the mask she wears, despite the walls erected around her, this tall woman with russet hair obeys the invisible laws that govern memory, feelings, and survival. She wants to know if Paloma has contacted the magistrate, if she has submitted her request for permission to visit, if she has news, if she has telephoned the warden of the detention center. She wants to tell her she has this morning sent a package to her with some of Wolf's clothes.

But Paloma does not pick up the phone. Phoenix goes out into the yard and looks up at the sky. Is it extraordinary if guilt, that monster with its honeyed tones (*you should have replied to Paloma's letters, your anger and pride are your undoing, you should have allowed Wolf to contact his sister, you should have allowed Paloma to talk to her brother, but you wanted your revenge and furthermore you should never have given him driving lessons, it's because of you he's in prison, you should have loved your children better*), bears down on her like the swarm of a thousand insects? She starts walking and her feet automatically follow the path laid down around the house and beneath this immense sky that she, unlike her son, can see. She begins running and here, on this path that Wolf followed so many times, there's something she would like to discover, but what? She keeps on running and begins to hope that if she doesn't stop, if she refuses to tire, she will end up putting time into reverse and catching sight of Wolf in front of her, that strange boy who runs in order to forget.

Wolf has slept for a good part of the afternoon and when he wakes up it is suppertime and still daylight. He says yes to what the detainee distributing the meal offers him. *Chicken nuggets? Yes. Zucchini? Yes. Cream cheese? Yes. Yogurt? Yes.* He hears all the doors opening and closing, people from one end of the corridor to the other being summoned in turn, and he analyzes all the sounds minutely, separating each one from the rest, in order to endure them better: the cart banging into the guardrail, the ladle tapping against the bowl, the creaking wheels of the same cart, the trays sliding over other trays, the glasses clinking together, the voices of the guard and the detainee saying the same things at each cell as it opens. *Chicken nuggets? Zucchini? Cream cheese? Yogurt? Bon appétit!* Wolf eats slowly, chewing the food as if he were squeezing it again and again to extract some kind of taste from it. He hands back his tray and after that dusk invades the prison with its hazy tint and its ghosts. It is the time of day when all dreads rise to the surface, when babies start to cry and adults sigh for no good reason. The air seems to break up into fragments and here, in this place, this lurch over the brink, which has struck fear into the hearts of men from time immemorial, becomes an abyss. Wolf stands up against the bars, as close as possible to the world.

Keep the heart closed, keep the heart closed.

From out of other galleries, from other corridors, through the bars, hands emerge waving scraps of white cloth. What is that for, Wolf wonders. To say that they are defeated, that they surrender? There are conversations, bursts of mocking laughter, insults, threats. When the night covers everything, when other guards have come on duty, when the sounds mingle together in the drafty corridors, there are some men who begin calling out the names of other prisoners and some the names of women. Yet there, in the night, all that these women's names have to offer is the emptiness of absence and the well of regrets. You need to be humble at such a moment, faced with this captive humanity, as it calls out, because it is now only voices that can pass through the bars. No hands, no caresses, no embraces.

The night advances like a tide, borne up by all these voices, then it holds its tongue and the silence is no better.

Several times the spyhole opens, someone says to him *You must sleep* but as it is neither his mother nor his sister nor a friend, the words remain outside the door, they do not reach him.

Perhaps he dozes off and once or twice he recognizes his own voice calling out. What is it calling?

A bird.

The new words

Paloma never expected to be doing so much talking during this first week, or that what would open up before her would be a vast, parallel world, hitherto unknown, one that she would like to be able to give a name to, as one gives a name to a country. It is a world that comes into existence when you have a family member in prison. She is learning new words and familiar words with new meanings: detainee number, *cantiner* (shopping in prison), *police judiciare* (criminal investigation department), visiting center, clerk of the court's office, *linge* (linen), what the authorities call clothing. She talks to people she does not know: the probation officer, who is called Marion, the warden of the detention center whom she addresses as Monsieur. She has written to the magistrate who remanded Wolf into custody. To all of them she has to say who she is (the sister, aged twenty-eight, unmarried, with no children), her occupation (a librarian for seven years), her status (tenant of a flat of fifty square meters located sixteen kilometers away from the detention center), her purpose (to visit her brother, to take clothing to her brother, to give her brother money so that he can shop at the center, to lend books to her brother, to get her brother out of prison). She talks to Dr. Michel, who is still in practice and promises a letter. The letter that reaches her two days later says that he brought Wolf into the world and sees him regularly. He writes that Wolf is a good boy who has his head somewhat in the clouds and is subject to anxiety attacks. Wolf, he writes in his doctor's handwriting, would not harm anyone and, of all the places on the earth, prison is the only one he would find it impossible to endure. Paloma doesn't agree and in her head she makes a list of all the other places Wolf would find it impossible to endure: a cellar, a hole, a hot air balloon, a desert island, under the sea, a haunted house, the hollow in their yard. She does this to shield herself from the extreme nature of Dr. Michel's words, which provoke a new upsurge of anxiety at not, in fact, knowing how Wolf spends his days, how he resists that cell, what he's thinking about, who he thinks about, who he speaks to and about what, how he holds his own when confronted by others who are less gentle, more hostile.

Every day she talks to Marion and when she confesses her anxiety to her, Marion tells her *He's quite calm, I've seen him, he's quite calm.* To Paloma this sounds as if she were talking about an animal under sedation. He's quite calm.

Paloma never expected to be talking to her mother every day, that week. These are simple conversations, ones that do not allow for silences between one sentence and the next, but nevertheless without an ounce of lies or pretense.

When Paloma learns that her request to visit has been granted, that she has an appointment in the visiting center for Friday at 2 p.m., her mother is the first person she calls and this time there is a silence between them that is compounded of relief and joy. Phoenix says *I'm glad* and Paloma holds on to this remark, as if it were a precious jewel that she must not allow herself to lose, and replies very softly, so as not to bring them bad luck, *So am I.*

The detention center is in a residential district and at first Paloma thinks she has the wrong address but no, there it is, at the far end of a road lined with single-family homes where, on this day in early summer, flowers are spilling out everywhere, climbing, flaunting themselves. As she walks along the sidewalk, swings, children's playhouses, and lawn furniture can be glimpsed through the hedges and when she sees all this Paloma thinks about the yard at her home back there, half-filled with spare parts and half-abandoned. She thinks about that hollow and this always has the effect on her of an ancient fear nuzzling against her arm. At the very end of the road there is the detention center and what's all that blue, that immaculate white, what's it doing there? Shouldn't it be gray or black to prepare people's hearts and minds? Paloma presses on, burdened with a duffel bag containing clothes for Wolf (any color except navy blue, to avoid confusion with the guards' uniforms), she is a good half-hour early but in this parallel country everyone who is up for the visiting center, as the phrase goes, comes early. There are only women there, of all ages, but they do not form a line. They talk, they smoke, they sit staring into space. Some of them are looking after their children in a tiny garden for relatives laid out beside the reception building.

Paloma does not go in and at moments like this when one is forced to look down, when one finds oneself rubbing shoulders with the invisible and the powerless, it is not always the milk of human kindness that guides us. Paloma would like to tell them loud and clear that she's there by chance, that she's not used to this, that she's not like them, these women whom she finds somewhat vulgar, somewhat obese, too heavily made-up . . . A young woman turns to her and stares at her openly, as if she had overheard her thoughts. Caught in her stare, Paloma is naked, exposed, weighed down by these unlovely reflections of hers and she is ashamed but what is to be done? One's heart needs to be scrubbed clean every day, at every challenge. As the time approaches the women slowly form into a line and the children go to hold their mothers' hands. Suddenly everyone there outside this detention center with its blue and white facade looks alike. Their hearts pound, their throats grow dry, their minds are in torment. When it is Paloma's turn she says her brother's name and his detainee number, she shows her documents, she puts her bag through a metal detector, she herself walks through a doorway like the ones at airports, and she is on the other side. Detainee 16587 is my brother, she keeps endlessly repeating in her head.

Where inside and
outside meet

It is a room reminiscent of a classroom at an elementary school because there is the same furniture with yellow metal legs. There are eight square tables, sometimes with two chairs at them, sometimes four. Paloma sits down at a table at the end of the room and outside there are prolonged beeping sounds, crackling sounds, the sounds of doors, keys, boots, gates sliding back, people calling out and others responding.

No, all that isn't outside, it's on the other side. It's inside, within the belly, and that is how Paloma pictures the prison at this moment, like an animal, and she is thinking of her brother walking toward her, in the entrails of this animal. It's a notion that somewhat embarrasses her; at her age she ought to be able to look at things as they are, picture them without turning them into a fairy tale, however horrible.

The color of the walls is hard to define. It may once have been white, or beige, or pale yellow, but then how could how can it be anything other than this color, which

113

seems to move with the light, to change when you move your head, to stare at you when you stare at it? This is the place where the outside world rubs shoulders with the inside, where desires are never fulfilled, where things are never fully said, and linger there on the walls, in the air.

Paloma was not expecting her brother to be the first one to come through the door, she had pictured herself waiting, being the last, growing impatient, but no, she has no time for any of that.

Wolf is there, accompanied by a guard, walking toward her and of course he's no longer the boy of seven whom she had left sitting at a table in front of a portion of Black Forest cake and to whom she had said *I'll come back and fetch you very soon.*

Wolf is tall, like their mother, he's beautiful, like their mother, and he's walking toward Paloma as if he were without fear, without expectation, but when he reaches her his eyes open wide and it looks as if there is something struggling to come out. What is it, a word, a thought, a tear, a child?

How can one compress ten years of waiting into a sentence that is both gentle and truthful, wonders Paloma, a young woman who takes up so little space in the world and who has retained from her childhood the habit of sitting quite still, very still, on the edge of a chair. What she would like to say to him wells up as a whole flood of thoughts, emotions, questions, feelings, it's all there in her throat and for heaven's sake, say something! Instead of opening her mouth Paloma compresses her lips, gulps, swallows, and Wolf, on the other side of the table, recognizes this expression, yes, this woman here is definitely his sister and he says:

"How's things, Paloma?"

"Oh, Wolf."

Wolf, she says, again and again, with tears in her eyes, as if, in place of a whole sentence, she had found a single word to evoke those ten years, a word both gentle and truthful.

They have half an hour and they do not say a great deal, unlike the others who are talking, asking, arguing, and touching. Paloma and Wolf have their hands placed flat on the table and this proximity is enough for them, they who have grown up with the distant love that their mother afforded them, a cautious love, a love that gave the impression it could take flight at the slightest noise. They know how to be content with this, seeing their hands side by side, and occasionally they smile at one another. When they have five minutes left Paloma tells him that he is due to appear before the magistrate the following Tuesday. Wolf nods, breathing heavily, he is shaking a little and Paloma is guessing at both the hope he still has and the suffering he feels at being here, as well as his response to the outside world of which, for now, he can catch only a glimpse.

"There is one thing, Wolf. Maman has to be there for the hearing. She's the one who has parental authority."

"She'll never want to come here. She hates this town."

"Yes, I know. But I think she'll come. For you."

*

And on this remark the last minutes pass in silence. There are embraces and promises and then Paloma is outside, very quickly, dazed by the light, by the cars, by the people walking quietly along, by the beautiful arrangements of flowers in the gardens, and by the sky, so blue above all this, like a lie.

What Wolf will never say

That he sometimes finds consolation in the workings of this machine where time is master. Getting up, having meals, and going to bed are at fixed times, he goes out twice a day for exercise in the yard, and, since the arrival of a letter from Dr. Michel at the detention center, he is allowed to spend an hour every afternoon running on a lawn (dawn, pawn) where his feet sink into the grass a little. Once the day begins he knows that the whole of it can go by without him, which is only a manner of speaking, of course, but is also a little bit true. His mind could be totally far away, in another country, in another era, or else utterly absorbed within him, deep within him, and his body would get on with its existence. He would be cleaning out his cell in the morning with a broom and a rag and the guard would be watching him out of the corner of his eye. He would be chewing his breakfast. He would be going to take a shower. He would be returning to his cell, which would not be opened again until lunchtime. His body would be there, of course, lying, standing up, sitting down, but his mind would be swimming, running, watching television. His body would become covered in red patches, he would scratch himself in his sleep, he would lose weight, he would no longer speak, but his mind would be twisting and turning like a great sail flapping in the wind.

He receives a visit from his probation officer who says *I'm very hopeful, your sister's working hard, things are looking good*. He is taken to a lesson a couple of times, given by a teacher who calls him *old chum*, but, as this man has been forewarned, he is left alone. He is even allowed to read comics. All the time he is afraid: of the adult detainees on the floor above, whom he can see and hear through the netting; of the ones in the cells next door to him; of the voices that pass through walls; of the night that seems to last an eternity; of the little flies that come in the evening and buzz around the light (fright, delight); of the hands spinning yo-yos from one cell to the next; of the faces, so many faces that appear through the bars; and, more than anything, of their eyes, all of them, so dark, so piercing. He is afraid of having to stay here for long. He is afraid of being forgotten, as he is so silent and invisible. He is afraid that this place will swallow him whole and never spit him out again.

The road back
the other way

As she made her way down to the gate in the small hours with pliers and wire cutters in her hand, Phoenix thought again about Fanny. That girl who lived in the abandoned van with her three dogs. She had a clear memory of the way those dogs used to stay close beside Fanny as she walked through the town or when she was doing her fortune-telling for a few euros. They had this trick of slightly lifting their heads toward people who came up to Fanny, in a manner that was extremely human, extremely threatening. Fanny was a mad devil, she would break into a dance or burst out laughing for no reason at all, but when she looked at Eliette her eyes grew dark, like those of sharks. Perhaps she really could read her future, perhaps it was all running past in her head and with her bottomless gaze she could see it: the fire, the madness, this house, the two children with no father. Perhaps she had had a presentiment of the loneliness and disarray of that very morning as, barefoot and dressed in a white nightgown, Phoenix tried to

take down the sign AUTO PARTS: OPEN MONDAY TO
SATURDAY.

She struggles furiously to cut through the wire but it is
thick and rusty, wound around the gate many times. She
has slept little during the night, thinking about the train
journey that awaits her, and about those songs she used
to sing in the yellow living room, those tight dresses that
constricted her, her face outrageously made-up, that man,
that Jean or Gérard who forced a kiss on her, and, across all
those years, the taste of tobacco and sweat had still come
back to her, and, oh ancient pain, she could once more feel
that ball in the pit of her stomach.

We must think about her body covered in depictions of
ivy, tendrils, dragons, phoenix. All things that climb sinu-
ously upward, take flight, make a show, because Phoenix
always dreamed of being like that. But today there is no
longer any room for such promises of earlier times. This
morning she tugs, she tears, she shakes at that sign, which
still does not give way, and a fit of wild rage, oh friend of
days gone by, wells up within her body.

She must be pictured throwing aside the pliers and the
wire cutter, running, still barefoot, to the garage, threading
her way over to the wall where the tools are kept, grasping
the hammer, going back to the gate, and battering away at
the sign with great blows until it splits, breaks, and finally
shatters and there is no one to hear her yelling, there in the
rosy pink of the dawning day, this Phoenix who looks like
a madwoman or a hysteric or simply a woman distraught
with grief.

She spends a long time taking a shower, washes her hair, plucks her eyebrows, tries on different earrings before choosing a pair.

She selects a long, plain, pale green dress, slipping it on over her head—a sudden memory comes back to her, of how her mother liked to hold a piece of fabric in her fingers, sometimes running it along her forearm, while thinking of what she might make with it—and she puts on ballet flats. She covers her tattooed arms with a long-sleeved jacket. She gives her lips just a faint touch of color. Before going out she decides to braid her hair. She is not aware of how magnificent she looks in this ankle-length dress, with the braid falling across her right breast and her almost bare, unwavering face that reveals nothing of what troubles her heart, exercises her mind.

Phoenix closes up the house and garage and makes a tour of the yard, walking along the well-trodden path. She stops for a moment beside the hollow, which is still just a hollow, she looks around, oh just like that, so as to take in everything at once, in a single look, almost to take it in her arms. She tries not to think of the many *nevers* that have punctuated these last years. I will never leave here, I will never take down that signboard put there by Noah, I will never go back to the town of C., I will never speak to Paloma again, I will never weep again. She padlocks the gate and walks away.

Despite being apprehensive over what will be decided for Wolf, Phoenix is still angry with him and perhaps a little with Paloma as well. But as she draws farther away from that house, initially on foot, before taking first one train and then another, she allows herself to think about the little girl she once was, that Eliette who used to play in a make-shift playhouse in her bedroom, and, curiously, she has the strange impression that she's about to rediscover her.

And during all the hours before the moment that she dreads, which still lies ahead, amid this anticipation, amid this absence, her heart is beating, her stomach is churning, and her mind is confusing what *is*, here and now, with what *was*, way back then, yesterday with tomorrow, what is possible with what is certain. But you have to stand up straight, if life has taught her anything it is this, you have to hold your chin thrust a little upward, your shoulders well back. This moment ticking away in her head, ticking away in all her being, with this crowd now coming toward her, all these faces, these clothes, these bags and still her heart beating, her stomach churning, her mind harping on and on *how will you recognize her, will you recognize her, what if she doesn't come, what if she's not there, it's ten years now, what will she be like* and then suddenly.

Things are never the way you pictured them, are they?

Their eyes meet a long way off, and it is the mother who moves toward the daughter because the latter is petrified— by this beauty, by the tide of emotions that hits her, by the weight of those ten years, by the difficulty of being her mother's child—and still that heart is beating, the stomach is churning, the mind is struggling to find appropriate words, but the truth is that something else is taking over and it looks like a beginning. Like something opening up, something that promises who knows what, as yet, who knows how, as yet, but the hope is that it will resemble affection and, for the moment, that is enough for them.

And on the other side of the town, behind the walls, at the end of a long corridor, behind a yellow door, in his cell, the son is standing up straight, too, and waiting, too, for them to come and fetch him for the hearing before the magistrate. Marion will be there, Paloma, his mother, and himself. Marion says he ought to say something, tell them why he did what he did, talk about his "plans for the future." Marion says his sister has prepared everything and his mother will be there. Marion says if everything goes well he could be out by this evening. Marion says many things about fines to be paid, guarantees, supervision, about keeping to the straight and narrow, but Wolf doesn't listen to all of it. He is wondering if the world outside has a particular smell. It's a question that has obsessed him since he's been in prison because here, he knows, everything has its own sound, its own smell. The gate, the door, the walls, the table, the chair, the bed, the mattress, the light switch, the light bulb, the underside of the chair, the floor close to the door, the floor close to the window. Will he carry all these smells around with him from now on, will his ear always remember the noise of his cell door, that of his hands rubbing against the bars, of the rustling of his hair against the sheet, of his own voice, at night, when he calls out? Eight days here and people who say you can get used to anything are liars.

One day for Wolf

And as she sees his face, still open and frank, but has to wait a little for his smile, for it does not come as readily as it used to, Phoenix wonders what those eight days have done to her son. As Paloma sees the red marks all over his neck and the little streaks of spots on his cheeks, she thinks about the rest of her brother's body, possibly covered with such stigmata as only days in prison can bring about, and his head, the inside of his head, how can one picture what that is like without feelings of sorrow and regret?

So perhaps this mother and daughter, as they stand there side by side, are smiling the kind of smiles that do not reach the eyes and Wolf, who has always known how to see behind the skin of faces, behind people's masks, recognizes this pasted-on smile and knows it is a snare. He notices his sister's pinched lips and the swelling vein on his mother's forehead, he sees their eyes empty of color, he could mimic them and reflect their own images back at them, like an old, tarnished mirror, but what would be the point? His heart is closed.

The hearing takes place in an office where there are six of them: Wolf, Marion, Phoenix, Paloma, the magistrate, and, in the corner, another woman who has her hands poised over a keyboard. Yes, in this country that attempts to smooth over the sharp edges of misfortune and grief, children and minors, young people, in fact, are received in an office like any other. On the walls are posters and children's drawings and what are they saying?

They are saying here are two people waiting in a bar at night leaning against the counter; they are saying here are two hearts as big as that and as red as that, up in the sky, below the hearts and the sky there is a child lying down among the flowers, possibly daisies. They are saying words: "thank you," "merry Christmas." They are saying a tall tree on which every branch has been drawn and every leaf, too, with all the veins and curves, and just by looking at the tree you can feel the wind and the noise it makes when it ruffles every leaf of every tree. Truly this outside world has quite a smell to it.

Wolf sits down in front of the magistrate but to begin with what he is looking at is the thin strip of yellow on the tip of his shoe. This is a ray of sunlight and he takes his time, this boy who has spent eight days in prison. In the eyes of the world eight days is almost nothing, but in prison the world is no more than a dream of long ago. So he is studying this ray and following it back upward, as if it were the thread by which he, Wolf, might gently, gradually, resume the course of his life. He draws this yellow, this brightness, this little sun, toward himself, or rather he follows it, as it traces a wandering line across the wooden floor of the office, sometimes quite flat, sometimes tortuous, and soon this ray of light reaches the window where there are no bars and Wolf has his face turned toward this outside world, towards this yellow radiance and he knows he will never be the same again.

The magistrate speaks to him. He is a man in a white shirt with tortoiseshell-rimmed glasses who looks like the kind of man you might find in any one of the offices in the town and, as he says, he reads the facts. This man is not much to look at but he knows this country's history well and he knows its prisons and the things that take place only within walls, the way thought is crushed, bodies are packed in, souls are diminished.

Of course Wolf remembers that night when he drove on and on, passed without mishap through all the tolls, and switched on one of those radio programs with people calling in to request their favorite music, or to tell boyfriends and girlfriends how much they were loved, how much their absence caused sadness, how much their presence brought joy. Wolf went on driving, he had filled up the tank as well. He knew how to do that, he'd seen his mother do it several times, actions like this were simple for him to absorb, all he had to do was to watch, it was like that at home when little things needed to be repaired, he knew how to do it without being told.

It is also true that fear had made its appearance once he had left the highway and from that point on the magistrate tells it best: driving on the wrong side of the road, a multiple vehicle crash, a serious accident only just avoided, his refusal to get into the car with the police, his attempted flight across open country.

Wolf had merely wanted to run in order to calm himself down, but he says nothing, what would be the point of repeating it all again? He listens to the magistrate speaking, he listens to Marion, to his mother and his sister speaking.

They say that they can offer guarantees, they speak of apologies regrets excuses, they offer documents, they talk of a life outside in which Wolf would be more closely supervised in the future. *Supervised,* says the magistrate. *What do you mean by that?* And in her hoarse voice, reminiscent of women who sing of sadness and the blues, Phoenix says *I'll make sure he doesn't take the car out on his own again.*

But I don't think that's the problem, madame, the magistrate retorts and for Phoenix it is like a blow to the stomach. She knows exactly what this man means, this man who, as he has said, only knows them through documents and the facts of the case, but who has understood that the problem was nothing to do with the car or the driver's license. It was the way she had brought up her children, or rather the way she had kept her children at arm's length. She looks at Paloma and for the first time she would be glad for a moment when she is gently sidelined, when people other than herself make the decisions, people other than herself do the worrying, lose their tempers, when people other than herself do what has to be done.

But instead of turning toward Paloma, the magistrate looks at Wolf.

Would you like to say something, Wolf?

At the same moment the sunlight climbs onto Wolf's shoe. Is there a connection between this warmth and the voice and the question? But he has never been asked for his opinion before, or at least very rarely. He has always been shielded from himself, shielded from other people. Is it so extraordinary that, after those eight days, he now feels himself to be sufficiently far removed from what he once was to be able to speak without shaking? And what he tells is a dream that he had in bed that Friday night and this is how Wolf tells it, with his words all mixed up and his habit of making words rhyme, this is how he tells it:

"I went to sleep in Paloma's room the one that Maman won't touch since Paloma went away. Maman doesn't buy Black Forest cake anymore and sometimes Maman pretends not to see that I sleep in Paloma's bed but she knows I do. I know she knows because sometimes when I go into Paloma's room it smells of Maman and it's a smell bell well that only belongs to her it's the scent of rust jasmine the earth in the yard and I know she's been there but I don't know what she does there maybe she goes there because she misses Paloma too but she never tells me that. I'm sleeping in Paloma's bed that night, I've had my session with Dr. Michel and I'm tired of the doctor telling me about how I was born how beautiful my mother was and how my sister who was still little was looking out of the window. I go to sleep and I wake up too soon and it's morning already but I'm in my room the one at the end of the corridor snore more. I can hear Maman in the kitchen

and I tell myself it's not late and I've forgotten if I ought
to go to the mechanics' training center or if I ought to go
as an apprentice to the garage in the town and I don't like
lying there thinking blinking winking about things I don't
like and the day passing like that, so I get up. The corridor is
short the corridor isn't like it was before it's very bright and
that dazzles me I can see the morning light shining through
the kitchen and reaching right up to my bedroom door.
That's not normal I've got the feeling I get when things are
not as they should be. I find it hard to breathe my hands
are sweating I want to run and I call out Maman and she
answers me I'm in the kitchen but I don't understand. Her
voice is right in my ear as if she was quite close beside me.
I go forward a step at a time I know that Paloma's room
is off to the right but her room's not there anymore the
sitting room's there now I don't know what's happened and
Maman appears. She says to me what's going on which is
what she always says when she sees me never hello never
how are you always what's going on. I remember how
Paloma always used to say hello my little wolf cub but that
was before the Black Forest cake break mistake and I say
Maman where's Paloma's room and she says whose room?
I ask again where's Paloma's room and she says who? Who
are you talking about? And my head's spinning I ought to
be going to the center or the garage I don't like being late
and my mother repeats who's Paloma? And I answer why
she's my sister and there in my ear she starts laughing as
if that was the best joke of the year and now I understand
that I have no sister. I go all around the house and there's no

trace of her not a photograph not a scent not a sound nothing and I call out very loud Paloma Paloma and in the end I wake up in her room and I don't know anymore what's true what's false what's a dream what's reality if I have a sister blister transistor or not, if I'd simply dreamed all that and hoped for all that. So then, you see, I took Maman's car in the middle of the night without saying anything because I couldn't bear anymore not knowing and I came here because sometimes you have to know in order to go on living."

A place like this

There are places like this which remain hidden to the world for years and it is only people in the know who know about them.

It was during those days when the light lingers and hangs on so strongly that the devil cannot find a dark corner to lurk in. The daylight is everywhere, stripping, laying bare, soothing, and this unending daylight no longer inspires any fear, or at least only very little.

Paloma had this place from her grandfather, he brought her here to fly a kite, and sometimes this slight, discreet young woman seems to hear her own voice as a child exploding into fine bubbles amid the sound of the wind and it's a sweet, happy memory.

Eliette knew this place as well but Phoenix doesn't want to recognize it, she says she's never been here although there's something she can feel scratching away inside her head, but it's still too soon for such memories.

Wolf walks slowly. This place is new to him but he is no longer an innocent in the world as he has always been.

He has endured those days and nights deprived of their affection, he has journeyed through the barren hours that fouled up his cell, he has tasted words that, when spoken looking at a wall, or into a corner, or standing in front of a locked door, no longer have any meaning. He has closed his heart. His mother and his sister are ahead of him. They keep turning back to look at him and he understands their very particular love for him, an imperfect, uneasy love. He tries to give each of them one of his old smiles but it is still not quite there, it is much too soon.

Once upon a time there was this place open to the sea, the earth, and the sky. Here each thing had a history and each thing held a promise. Wolf savors each thing one by one, with his body, his face, his outstretched hands, and his mouth, too. It seems to him as if there can never be enough of such offerings and that a whole lifetime in this vast world will not suffice to speak of them all, to hold them all.